UNTHOLOGY 6

UΠTHANK
BOOKS

First published in 2015
By Unthank Books

Printed in England by Imprint Digital UK

ISBN 978-1-910061-04-6

Edited by Ashley Stokes and Robin Jones

Book and jacket design by Robot Mascot
www.robotmascot.co.uk

www.unthankbooks.com

Heaven on Earth

When jewelled saints
appear in your dreams

When the sky is absent
and life must be present

Then where is heaven if not here?

– Rebecca McManus

CONTENTS

INTRODUCTION

The Editors

All You Can Eat

Unthology 6 marks four years since the publication of Unthank Books' first anthology of shorter prose: *Unthology 1*.

In the intervening time we have witnessed many changes in the world of publishing as a whole but perhaps not quite as many in the world of short story collections. Four years ago we were generally aware of a vogue for very short or 'flash' fiction; a scarcity of major UK writers being discovered via their debut collections; a tendency to eschew experimentation in form and style, as well as a possible decline in the ability of the audience to even read longer short stories. This was the prevailing atmosphere that we established the *Unthology* series to counter. With it we aimed to publish as varied a spread of the short form of prose as was feasible. We welcomed novel extracts, we relished realist studies, we applauded the adventurous, and in keeping with some mantra we held to in our first year largely because it was assonant with 'Unthank,' we championed the 'unpredictable' and 'unconventional.'

Unthology 6 retains all of the spirit of the original with what we hope are a few upgrades. We have the second of what will be eventually three pieces by one author, which, Krzysztof Kieslowski-like, are simply named after primary colours. We have intimate relationship stories ranging from excoriating analysis to even-handed enquiry. We have the devastating follow-up story to a 'hit' from *Unthology 3* called *Even Meat Fill*. We even have, (yes there's too many 'evens' in this paragraph), shock of shocks, 'boyfriend falls on walking holiday.'

Five collections later since 'U1', change the world of short stories we have not, but we have noted a definite increase in the quantity and quality of submissions we receive for each collection such that we are now publishing twice yearly in the spring and autumn rather than annually. We remain convinced that the *Unthology*'s remit of no restrictions on word count, theme or author-profile provides a genuinely popular space for short-form prose to proliferate and prosper i.e.: work chosen entirely on merit and interest. On the plus side for us the editors, such a heterogeneous mix of writing makes it very easy for us to align arresting arrays of delicious fare, and finally we hope you the readers continue to be tempted by our 'all-you-can-eat buffets' and that they always turn out to be eminently edible, if not banquets.

PSYCHO-NASAL AGGRAVATION SYNDROME

Gordon Collins

I check myself in the mirror. My sullen brow and my lightly speckled complexion season my face with the mystery of age, but my lips have retained some fullness, my eyes some enthusiasm and my tied-back hair, although streaked with grey, is thick and playfully long. I'm handsome and she'll say yes.

Who would have thought that, after all we have been through, it would come to this: a mutual acceptance and a proposal of marriage. It's been a hard journey – Laura and I have been at each other's throats ever since we met. But that's all done with now. I am confident that our problems are behind us, for – I see it so clearly now – I have finally dealt with their cause: nose hair.

It was four years ago that I discovered them. I stood in front of the bathroom mirror: head tilted back, eyes glaring, teeth clenched, rim of nostril flared, gripped and levered open to expose a bed of nails – a dark mesh of hairs completely covering the nasal membrane and receding deep into the cavity.

'It's normal. Haven't you seen that before?' Laura said when I woke her.

'You knew about this?' I screamed at her and from this, we concocted a monstrous row. At first, she stood her ground, arguing that it wasn't her responsibility and it was just natural anyway. I listened to her calmly and then methodically deconstructed her arguments by recalling the 'respect' clauses in the relationship contract we had both signed, invoking the mutual responsibilities we had subscribed to and asserting that her ignorance was no defence. She wasn't really listening. She became quite emotional. I patiently waited until she calmed down and then went through my arguments again and again until, thankfully, she ended up apologising in the early hours of the morning.

Then I made her examine me head to toe, and list all the rogue sproutings, the hidden fuzzes and unchecked bristles that she could find on me. I spent the rest of the morning contorting myself while holding a hand mirror and checking against old photographs for other unexpected growths. By lunchtime, I had confirmed all of her reports and a few others and had a page-long inventory of my body hair, the highlights of which were:

- A fine white hair growing 3cm directly out of my forehead
- Toe beards
- 1.2cm long hairs on each earlobe
- A fleecy covering on my shoulders
- Some other growth that I won't describe here

Over the next few months I managed to accept these as a dignified part of aging, a sign of wisdom and a demand for respect. For what could be more authoritative than a beard, whether it be on the chin, the toes or the chest? If it came down to it, I could prove I was a man to be listened to and not some bald-backed fool. In the summer, I could frame my 10 bearded philosophers in a sandal while younger men would hide their baby-faced toes in their childish trainers. In the winter, my arse would have the warmth of the wise.

I left my body clothed in the fleece that God intended for it. I maintained a healthy beard and, up until about six months ago, I luxuriated in its cosy warmth and postured behind its façade of respectability.

But then I got some genetic freak of a thick dark greasy nose hair which was probably caused by too much wheat in my diet or something and which uncompromisingly grew straight out of one side of my nostril and burrowed into the other as if in a desperate escape attempt. I had to have several goes at it with my tweezers until I pinged it out and installed it in pride of place on the mantelpiece in My Museum of Myself next to the other freaky exhibits: a huge toe nail and a piece of ear wax that looks like a totem pole.

But that was not the end of it. As well as nasal extremists, other freaks appeared on my nipples, my genitals and my eyebrows. They too were ripped out as examples to the rest, and measured and catalogued but more and more came back, especially in the nose area. I plucked them all. I spent hours here in front of the mirror, plucking, snorting and rinsing. I was obsessed. I let it get to me and, of course, I was not able to stop myself taking it out on Laura. I started up on her about it at the slightest excuse. She – nasally alopecic – couldn't empathise at all. She couldn't see what it was doing to me. I, well, I couldn't differentiate my nasal irritation from irritation with her. I mean, why would she interrupt me when I was plucking? How does saying, 'Calm down,' help? We fought and fought.

I believe that it was this, perhaps on top of some residual upset from our big argument on that night of discovery and perhaps some disgust at what was happening to me but, yes, it was mostly my nasal hair problem that was to blame for Laura leaving me. She didn't realise this, of course. She said it was because I was too controlling, intolerant, didn't listen – the usual stuff. She sees things emotionally and not as cause and effect, you see. That's what got her into trouble before with the jewellery shop and her pottery studio and all her projects that end up with me bailing her out at great expense. If she was just a bit more thoughtful herself, I mean if she'd only think about things more, then she would have seen that our problems were not so much emotional as nasal.

Like I say, I've forgiven her now. I can understand that her first impulse was to panic and leave and not consider that we might tackle my problem together. Perhaps that was too much to ask. After all, my particular affliction, although common, has not been well reported. I couldn't really expect her to understand what was happening to me deep in that dark cavern. I suppose I was destined to suffer on my own for a while. It all turned out well in the end, though. We've been fortunate, but it hasn't been easy for me and, at times, I could have done with some support from her.

Anyway, around this time, she left me to myself with my irritation and my nasal passage in tatters from too much weeding and the problem only worsening as the shoots came back time after time. Now the issues came sharply into focus. My plucking strategy wasn't working but letting them grow was unbearable. There was only one other option. And yet, when I stood here in front of the mirror, my nostril wedged wide open, oriented it towards the light and in my hand a state-of-the-art, fresh-out-of-the-box, nasal hair trimmer held at the recommended angle prepared for attack, I knew it was wrong. I knew I was defiling myself but it was too late.

I got carried away. The more the hairs flew out of my nose, the more frenzied I became. I was soon ignoring the 5mm intrusion limit recommended by the manufacturer and had it right up as far as it would go, twisting, prodding, dragging it like a lawnmower and, after twenty minutes, I had a full harvest from both nostrils with an average length of 3mm. It was a massacre.

Suddenly I was no longer a hairy conk. I was clean-shaven. It was a victory over my hirsutity, if you'll permit me. I was a bald-nose. I ponced about for the rest of the day. I went out and bought clothes that were too young for me. I dined at new restaurants and pretended to be gay. I called up old friends and got fantastically smashed. We gatecrashed parties and went to nightclubs. I felt up young girls and propositioned slightly older ones and I don't know how I got home.

Then, the day after, this flush of youth mellowed and was replaced by a wonderful, smooth calm, which I filled with Elgar and walks on The Common. Those weeks that followed were blissful. I was creative and bold, just like my days at college. I was a better person; contented. I was myself. My friends called me every day and I was communicative and open with them. I built the foundations of a forgiveness of my father. I read books. I flirted with vegetarianism. Freed from my obsession, as I was then able to see it, I was happy.

I even called Laura. She took some convincing but I persevered and eventually managed to sound so desperate that she agreed to go out with me for dinner. That night, in the restaurant, I admitted to her that I must have been impossible to live with but that I had mellowed now and had come to find my true being. I demonstrated the annoyance of nasal growth by using an old toothbrush on her own delicate proboscis. I told her what a difference nasal shaving had made in my life. I told her about the possibilities I saw for us and I suggested we start again, like we'd just met but this time there would be a new era of listening. I think she was coming round to my point of view when I felt something twitch deep inside my nose. I excused myself and went to the bathroom.

In the mirror, I saw them. They had come back but now they were thicker and denser. I scratched, I plucked, I tweaked, I rearranged. How could they have grown back so quickly? I returned to the table and tried to ignore them. Laura was saying something about, 'portals into the world of possibility' but I couldn't listen because the irritation was too distracting. I ran out to the 24-hour pharmacy but they didn't stock nasal hair trimmers. They did sell me a tube of soothing ointment with a picture of a fern on it, though. I emptied it into both nostrils and returned to the restaurant where she was saying something like, 'I'm now in a place where I can...' but I had to stop her because the cream was dripping out of my nose into my pasta and it wasn't working anyway. I went back to the bathroom to have a proper excavation but with nothing better than angry pudgy fingers as an implement it took a good thirty minutes to pluck them all out to my satisfaction. When I got back to the table she was gone, leaving only a note on the napkin about how nothing had changed and not to call her, ever. 'Never call me again!' I think it was.

After that, I was shaving every day. Peering and shaving and plucking but I never seemed to get them all out. I thought I had, but there would always be another guerrilla hiding, curled up by a sinus perhaps, at the back of the cave waiting for the patrol to go so it could come back out and counterattack. The irritation never stopped. I tried everything. I bought all sorts of curved tweezers, adjustable clipper attachments, minute razors and even an imported fibre-optic-camera-guided burner. Nothing worked. I tried naked candle flames, potent acids and solvents, extremely hard nose blowing and a special strain of hair-eating lice. I tried plucking through exploratory incisions. I tried to catch them out by waking in the middle of the night and plucking, or plucking while driving. I tried shaving upside-down, underwater, after hours of massage – Scandinavian and Indian nasal. I tried shaving after flushing with olive oil, baby cream, tomato sauce, wet clay. No joy.

I consulted four different GPs; they all fobbed me off with some placebo cream or counselling or a consultation with some half-witted teenage intern who told me that noses weren't his speciality. Counselling! I pored over medical journals. I spent days on the Internet. I saw holistic therapists who recommended that I calm my mind but, 'How can I be calm when there's a pin cushion in my bloody nose?' I pointed out to them.

In all my research one name cropped up again and again: Dr Salan, a consultant in the Ear Nose and Throat department at St George's. I called him but was told he didn't see patients since he was too busy with his research into something called

'PNAS'. He wouldn't reply to my emails and the receptionist denied any knowledge of him and so I wandered the strip-lit corridors of St George's Hospital, avoiding the parked wheelchairs, the dribbling infirm and the laughing nurses until, deep inside building 'J' I found his name on a door.

In fact Dr Salan, a short Middle-Eastern fellow, was more than happy to examine me. He was immediately peering up my nose. With my head back I could survey his room – piles of papers, monitors, swabs, bandages, scrubs, waxing kits and tiny spidery things that I took to be nose wigs. There was a range of instruments on heavy wheeled stands that had been herded into the corner. Each one had a different drill on an adjustable stand. Each one was a larger version of my nasal hair trimmer.

'Ah. Yes. Earlier extremities may have encouraged further... a classic case... very good... self-treatment has only aggravated...' He shook his head vigorously, 'Very amateurish. You've been at it with a trimmer, I see.'

'Yes. How...'

'Did I know? How did I know? How did I know? The characteristic n-shaped bristle ends, the chaffing at the nostril entrance, how, how, how. I've been doing this for long enough to recognise a messed-up hooter. Have you found yourself getting irritated at little things recently?'

'Yes, I –'

'Any insomnia, shouting at inanimate objects, self harm?'

'Yes, yes, I –'

'I don't know why I bother asking. It's as clear as the proverbial, a classic case of PNAS.'

'PNAS?' I asked.

'Of course, typical, very much of course. I shouldn't be surprised. "It's not in the public sphere," they say. 'Not a fashionable disease', 'not a funding priority' and so I'm left here, the only doctor in London who is researching these cases, these serial pluckers, torchers, nasal fetishists and rhinotillexomaniacs. Did you know that I have diagnosed

10% of the hospital community with PNAS? It's practically an epidemic and yet...'

'Alright! You've made your point. Can you, please just tell me what's wrong with me!' How could I have? How could I shout this way at this kind man who would come to be my saviour?

'Yes, right. PNAS. Psycho-Nasal Aggravation Syndrome. Well, here's the thing. Your nose hairs have an important role in filtering out dust in your inhale, but you probably didn't realise that they perform a dual function, yes, yes, yes, in fact, they lie proximal to a group of nerves which have a direct connection to a part of the brain known as Bracknell's Capsule which, CT scans tell us, is the part of the brain responsible for receiving and processing irritation.'

He brought out a large board with a diagram of a human head on it. He ran his finger along a dark line that went from a red light bulb in the front of the brain to the back of the nose and continued into a piece of black string that came out of the board at the nostril.

'It is believed that our nasal hairs act as sensors which are finely tuned to detecting irritation and hence, as those in the Nasal-linguistics field suggest, lead to expressions such as "Getting up your nose" or "Tweaking the bristle".'

He snorted five times in rapid succession. I wondered if this was his laugh.

'In any case, shaving, plucking or, God forbid, burning or worse, no, no, this would be the equivalent, in the irritation sense, the equivalent of poking your eyes out. Irritation blindness may be a useful term for you.'

He pulled the string on the diagram and the red light came on. He smiled excitedly.

I felt a twitching in my nose again. 'Will those do the job?' I said pointing at the wheeled-trimmers in the corner. They were prickling again, making me mad. 'I'm not leaving here until you shave my nose!' I kicked up a fuss but he just laughed at me. He was quite used to dealing with the tantrums of a PNAS sufferer.

'You think you can shave your way out of chronic irritation? No. No. No. I am afraid there is only one effective treatment. A quite radical procedure I have pioneered but I am not allowed to recommend it unless you ask about it.'

'What is it?'

'What is what?'

I sniffled. I grabbed my nose and pulled it hard. 'Tell me about the radical treatment you stupid little man!'

*

Looking back I feel nothing but shame. I can't believe I acted like that. Dr Salan was right of course. I love that man. What he did for me… Well, he saved me from myself. To think that I would hate myself so much.

We found a way to live together, my hairs and I. The trimmer and all the other weapons of suppression have gone back to the shops, and legal proceedings against their manufacturers have been initiated. My personal Museum of Myself has closed – it was an exploitative freak show. I am studying PNAS along with Dr Salan in an effort to raise awareness. It's an uphill struggle but we will get there.

It's been hard but I have learnt something important: tolerance breeds tolerance. Soon after I stopped fighting them, they stopped fighting me, and the irritation at last ceased. With Laura too. Soon to be my fiancé. I begged her to give me one last chance and I was able to convince her that we could at last work together and this time from a position of mutual acceptance. She, well, she had got into trouble with her credit cards again and needed my help and so the timing was perfect.

It's all due to Dr Salan and his radical treatment – a complete nasalectomy to free the hairs, to let them flow out of my face into the world and not be imprisoned where they only prickle and plot and agitate.

I check myself one last time. I loosen the clasp on my ponytail. I'll wear my hair down tonight. I take a pinch of wax and, lightly but assertively, grab the two eccentric locks of hair, which spring out five centimetres from the holes on my face. I caress them thoughtfully. I haven't shown them to her yet; I've worn them tied up under the bandages until now. I'm sure she can come to love them too, though, for they are now a symbol of what we have achieved, a symbol of tolerance.

In the mirror I see a man who has found a way to love himself. A man, for whom this has not been easy, and yet, for all their difficulty the lessons have been more thoroughly learnt. A man who, if he has not aged well, he will, from now on, age better. A man with no nose but instead, a cascade of thick glossy hairs flowing from the middle of his face.

With a snap of my fingers, I twist them up into a gloriously flowing moustache.

THE STORY WITH YULIYA HAS A BAD ENDING

Alexandros Plasatis

What sort of café frappé is this, Pavlo, man? If I hold the glass near the lamp I can see through it – see? Say that again? Ah… It sort of settles after a couple of hours… Right. Make me another one. One and a half spoons of sugar, six drops of milk. Strong. Very strong. And bring me a jug of water with ice. I'm thirsty. Make the frappé very strong, eh? These bloody mosquitoes fuck my evening. Tell your boss he must do something about these bloody mosquitoes. And it's so hot, man!…You know, Pavlo, why don't you quit polishing those glasses and bring your stool closer? I want to tell you the story with Yuliya. Do you remember her? Pffff… What a woman, eh? Russian… We used to come here sometimes for ouzo and meze. Really? You remember everything? What? OK, OK. Later. Don't forget the jug of water…

Pavlo doesn't want to listen. He says he's busy. What the hell, I'm going to tell him the story with Yuliya anyway.

Listen, man. She was such a beautiful woman, Russian, you know, tall, blonde. We were living together at my place. In my flat. I wanted to marry this woman. I knew. I understood.

Me Egyptian, her Russian. Different cultures. You see, I let her sometimes go out for a coffee with her girlfriends, but why did she have to *work*? *I* was working as a fisherman at the time. OK, yes, we went out together, sometimes she'd come here to the café with her girlfriends, drink coffee, have ouzo, you know, nice, civilised stuff. But why did she have to work in a *bar*?

DON'T JUST STAND THERE! MAKE MY COFFEE! I'M THIRSTY!

I don't know, Pavlo, sometimes you're so slow... You aren't dumb or anything and that's why I talk to you, but sometimes you're so slow, mate. I'm sitting here at the bar because I don't like the other Egyptians. Only one or two of them are real men. The rest talk behind your back. They say I've done *things* back in Egypt and that's why I never go home. They can fuck off. Look at them, man, look at them, sitting around that table... miserable... hunched over their beer... one hand in their pockets so as not to lose their money... talking about the job on the trawlers... They only care about money. Trawlers, trawlers, trawlers, trawlers. Fuck you and your trawlers. I'm sick of the trawlers...

Nice one, Pavlo. Thanks. That's fine. Keep the change... No problem, I won't keep topping it up with water and ice, it loses its colour, all right, I won't, whatever you say. You want a cigarette? Here, have one of mine. Yes, bloody mosquitoes... Come on, man, stop that polishing, it makes me dizzy. That's the third time you've polished the glasses. You look gay with that cloth in your hand. I told you to bring your stool closer. I'm not going to fucking bite you. I want to tell you the story with Yuliya... What do you mean you've heard millions of stories, man? You're a bar tender, that's part of your job. I'm not like the others who come here and tell you their bullshit and break your balls just because they've nothing better to do: 'Oh... I miss my country... Oh I lost my job... Oh my girlfriend, oh my mummy, oh my grandma...' No, man. Morning, noon, night, I always think of the story with Yuliya. Listen, do you remember when Yuliya and I used to come here? What a woman! Yes, yes, of course. Later…

He says he's busy. Bullshit… The waitress is doing everything. All he's doing is opening a bottle of beer and making a lousy coffee now and then, and putting them on her tray. And washing a glass or two every ten minutes. Right…

You see, Pavlo, Yuliya left me because she was scared. She left me and she fled the town. And she thought that I couldn't find her. Now, did she *really* think that I couldn't find her?

I get hold of her number…

Bloody hell… I told him to make a strong frappé. What's wrong with him?

What's that coffee, boy? What's wrong with you? You call this thing strong? No, man. The fact that I'm tense doesn't prove that your coffees are strong. I'm always tense, for fuck's sake. No, I don't want a fucking chamomile tea! Put those aspirins up your arse. Never mind. Fuck it… I'll drink this one…

Where was I…?

So, yes, Yuliya leaves Kavala and thinks that I can't find her, but I get hold of her number. I call her. Once she listens to my voice, she shits in her pants. 'Look,' I tell her, 'are you trying to hide from *me*? What are you scared of, sweetie? I'm not going to hurt you. Come back and we'll talk it through. Nice, civilised stuff. Why did you leave like that?'

She didn't want to come back. I told her again, 'Don't be scared,' but she didn't want to come back.

Why, sweetie?

I find out from my guys, you know, the undercover officers, I know lots of undercovers, they're nice people, they're my friends (by the way, Pavlo, they know that you're a hashish smoker…), so I find out from my guys that Yuliya ran away to Sparta and got a job there. In one of those, you know, bars.

Sparta, eh?

I go to see her friends. Two Ukrainian girls. They used to work together.

I say, 'You working today?'

They say they aren't.

'Then let's go and find my girl.'

'Where is she?'

'Sparta.'

'Haha! Are you crazy, Rasool? Go to Sparta? How can we get from Kavala to Sparta tonight?'

'Get in the car and don't worry.'

We get in the car. Sit comfortably. We begin. The roads aren't busy and I've got this special light on my plates so that the cameras can't read them. Because I go fast. Very fast. Bullet-fast. I pass by Salonika. Pass Thessaly. Pass Lamia. Going down down down. All the way down. Man! The girls saw Greece from end to end in six hours or so… Yes, of course, it's fucking possible, man, I've done it, we left Kavala in the evening, approached Athens at night.

When I'm near Athens my phone rings. It's one of my guys, an undercover. He hasn't seen me for some time and worries about me. He probably thinks, 'What's going on with Rasool?'

He says, 'Hey man. Where are you?'

I say, 'I'm here. Where are you?'

He says, 'Well, I'm here, too.'

I say, 'Good. I'll come by later on.'

I switch off my mobile and drive past Athens.

Now, what happens next is this: Mohammed with the One Arm passes by the café and my guy asks him about me. One Arm has heard that I've left for Sparta and tells him so.

'SHIT!' my guy says, 'CRAZY RASOOL IS OFF TO SPARTA!'

He goes straight to the police station. He says, 'Oi, lads! Anyone got contacts with undercovers in Sparta? WE NEED TO STOP RASOOL BEFORE HE REACHES SPARTA.'

They find a contact. They call the contact. They say so and so. They say Rasool this and Rasool that. They pass on my details, the details of my car, and ask the Sparta contact to take care of me because I lose my temper easily, but I'm a nice lad really. They say to their contact that under no circumstances the police should let me inside the bar that Yuliya works in.

And I'm driving. Fast. It's night and I'm driving bullet-fast. With the two girls in the backseats. I enter Peloponnese. I see the sign for Sparta.

I'll find you, sweetie.

And just on the edge of Sparta, I see a police roadblock. As soon as I see the roadblock, Pavlo, I say to myself, 'This has something to do with my guys. They're trying to protect me.'

The police stop me.

I get out of the car.

I say, 'What's up, lads?'

They look at my plates. 'Where are you coming from?'

I tell them.

'Long time since we saw a car from up there in Sparta. Why're you going to Sparta?'

'Vacation. See Sparta. Just me and the girls. Is that bad?'

They let me go.

I reach Sparta.

I reach Sparta… Fuck. I need to find the bar now. Where could it be? I don't know Sparta. The girls don't know Sparta. We don't know the name of the bar. We don't know where to find it.

I know *how* to find it.

'Watch out for policemen,' I say to the girls.

I drive around the town centre.

'POLICE, POLICE!' scream the girls, 'POLICE, POLICE!'

Fucking hell. They almost made me deaf…

'Why are you screaming, sweeties?'

'Rasool! Be careful of the police, Rasool.'

I drive near the police. I park.

'What are you doing, crazy Rasool?'

'Don't worry, sweeties.'

I get out of the car.

The policemen come over to me.

'What's up, lads?' I say.

'Where are you going to?'

'I'd like to have a drink. In a bar. I'm on vacation, you see. Just me and the girls.'

'Do not enter the bar.'

'Which bar?'

'That bar.'

'Oh *that* bar? But why? Look, guys. We aren't going to do anything wrong. Just one drink. Nice, civilised stuff. Just me and the girls.'

'All right,' they say. 'But we'll be waiting outside. If anything happens, if *anything* happens, we'll take you straight to the police station.'

'Nothing will happen. Don't worry.'

They let me go.

We enter the bar.

Yuliya sees me and, man!... She shits in her pants.

She's behind the bar. She says something to her boss.

The boss comes over to me.

I say, 'I'm not talking to you. I want the girl.'

'The girl can't come over. She's busy.'

I say, 'I've nothing to say to you. Send over the girl.'

'I told you she's busy.'

I say, 'LOOK... I'M NOT GOING TO SAY IT AGAIN. I WANT *HER* TO SERVE ME. *HER!*'

'I'll send you another girl.'

'I want *her*.'

'Can't send her.'

And he goes to grab me.

'DON'T YOU FUCKING TOUCH ME OR I'LL SMASH UP YOUR FUCKING BAR.'

He goes to jerk me out of my seat and I jump up and push him off and smash whatever's in front of me and throw tables and kick chairs and chuck ashtrays and shout: 'I'M GOING TO KILL YOU, YULIYA! DON'T YOU KNOW IT?'

Police come in.

They grab me.

They take me to the station.

They say Yuliya will sue me.
They say her boss will sue me.
They say they'll get me a lawyer.
But this doesn't matter, cause they say I'll go to prison anyway.
I make a phone call.
They change their mind.
They say they know I'm a nice lad really.
They say I must leave Sparta first thing tomorrow morning.
They say, '*You* must leave Sparta first thing tomorrow morning.'
That's what they say.
'I'll come back here after I've killed her.'
That's what I say.
But they let me go.
I find a hotel for the girls to sleep.
I don't sleep.
I wait for the morning.
Morning comes.
I wait for the night.
Night comes.
I put the girls in the car. Drive past the bar. Slowly. It's closed. I get out of the car. Approach the bar. It's dark.

I press my face up against the window. It's pitch black, there's no one there.

The girls say they need to go back to work. They say they're tired.

I press my hands against the glass to stop the glare of the reflections.

Where are you, sweetie?

The girls want to go back home. They moan.

My nose bends against the glass.

Don't be scared, sweetie.

The girls moan. They need home.

I press harder against the glass, I feel it on my lips, I press harder, harder, my lips flatten against the glass – and I stay like that, staring into the darkness…

'Oh, Rasool, Rasool!' scream the girls.

And I see a shadow moving… It moves quickly, from one corner to the other, as if someone is sliding along the floor.

I go to the door. It's locked. I smash the lock, get inside. I can't find the light switch. I feel my way in the darkness, stamping my feet on the floor: 'Yu-uuuuliya… Are you trying to hide from me, Yuliyaaaaa?'

I hear a screech. I feel pain on my calf. It's a sharp pain. I get my lighter, strike it, look down. It's a cat. I'd stepped on her tail. Her teeth have sunk into my flesh. She won't let go. I kick her away.

I sit down, light a cigarette. I need to think. The cat comes to me, bites my other calf. She's a fucking crazy cat. I kick her away. She comes back. She's nuts. I grab her from the neck, strike my lighter. I bring the flame near her face, she stares at me, she shows me her teeth, hisses, she makes to scratch my face with her claws. I walk around, with the cat in my hand. Her flesh feels soft and warm in my grip, I like it. I walk, feeling my way in the dark. I come across a freezer. I open the freezer door, shove the cat in, shut the door.

I sit down, smoke.

The girls call out to me, 'Please, Rasool, please get out of there. Please let's go back.'

'Don't worry, sweeties. I just need to think for a moment.'

I finish my smoke, get in the car, we leave Sparta.

When we're near Athens, I stop the car. I turn around, drive back.

'What are you doing, Rasool?'

'I forgot the cat in the freezer.'

'What cat?'

'I put a cat in the freezer. I must get her out of there.'

'Please don't talk like that, Rasool. Please, you scare us.'

'You don't need to be scared, sweeties… I put a little cat in the freezer because she annoyed me. I've got to get her out.'

'Oh, don't talk like that, Rasool…'

I think of the cat's flesh. I drive fast. How soft she was, man… How warm she was, that's what I think. How warm and how light and I drive very fast, bullet-fast, and I enter Peloponnese again and the girls scream and I pass Corinth and they cry and I pass Argos and Tripoli, and take the exit for Sparta.

I'm coming, little kitten. I'll save you, I'll give you to Yuliya…

I reach Sparta. I find the bar. Park. I enter the bar, open the freezer.

The cat is frozen.

'Girls, can you write Russian?'

'Yes, we can, Rasool.'

I ask them to write down: *Yuliya, I'm sorry about this.*

I stick the note with the Russian writing on the freezer and we leave Sparta.

…And that's it, Pavlo, that's the story with Yuliya…

Well, say something, man…

What is it? I want the truth. I don't know, mate, nothing extraordinary happened in the end. What about the cat? She was fucking crazy, I didn't give a shit about her. No, I didn't eat the girls on the way back, I'm not like that. Yuliya is still in Sparta.

You don't like the ending?

Fucking hell, man, you're right. Yuliya is still in Sparta…

Pour me something strong now, a whisky. It's going to be a long night.

EGOR

Daisy Lafarge

1.

We are probably the two tallest people in the room. This is because we are not native to this country. He is from Russia and I am here by accident.

The room is lined with beautiful prints that make me want to pursue a more aesthetic life, despite previous failed attempts. The attention of people in this room is largely devoted to circumnavigating the prints and encountering acquaintances in similar attire to themselves.

Speeches are made in the local tongue by people in two-piece outfits as tiny cups of wine begin to orbit the room, held aloft by the hand of the only other twenty-something I can see.

Characteristically typical of being unable to gauge the direction of the middle-aged current, I commence an anti-clockwise, then clockwise, then cross-room inspection of the prints. This incurs the unspoken annoyance of several well-dressed older women who are probably more put out by my unwrinkled presence. I try to tell myself this is hardly my problem.

My eyes are set in the direction of the prints and to all appearances I am looking at them. In reality I am thinking about:

The original function of the gallery. The upper classes began to put on weight and so in order to exercise without being seen to sweat by the outside world, lined corridors with portraits so that they had something to look at whilst pacing back and forth. That in extremely cold climates in the north of this country, the birch trees have adapted to grow horizontally across the surface of the ground, skimming on silver bellies like snakes in order to avoid the extreme winds and cooler temperatures above ground.

The prints take inspiration from Italian landscapes and the preparatory drawings of Leonardo da Vinci. I wonder if I have failed to engage with the works at all or if my engagement with them has sparked a different kind of thought process.

For the past twenty minutes I have been dimly aware of the two dark eyes following me around the room. I camouflage my sideways glances at him by squinting to look at the prints. He is dressed as inappropriately as me but in a more dad-like way. He has not removed his blue sports puffa in spite of the warm inside temperature.

I hover opposite him by a table with publications where we both pretend to peruse the catalogue. I wander aimlessly to another print when he appears beside and above my left shoulder. Usually in this situation one of us is inclined to make a placid remark about the print, which would legitimate his proximity to me, and I am surprised by its arbitrary lack and by what happens instead.

He moves his body at a right angle to me and furrows his brows, which are dark with flecks of grey like the rest of his hair. First addressing me in the country's language and then English on seeing my apologetic shrug, he articulates slowly:

'Are you from here?'

'No.'

'Do you work here?'

'No, I study.'

'Do you like it?'

'There are not enough people here. Or, there are, but -'

'Yes there is not enough. That is why I come here. To be in filled rooms.'

'Mm.'

He is speaking strangely but I think I understand. The town is full of people that do not go outside or smile or talk. The people in this room seem terrible but I am grateful to be somewhere so well lit and busy.

'I would very much like to draw you.'

'Okay.'

'So we can meet?'

'Okay.'

'It is good to be with people.'

'Mm.'

I look around at the orange room, now hazy with the grey smears of the guests. They are all too busy with wine and a language I don't understand to notice that two lonely, bored foreigners are having a conversation. In a few minutes I have to leave to meet a friend at the station. The man asks me when I will be free. I give him my email address. I am not attracted to him but bored and lonely and only here by accident. I have had little opportunity to behave in a way that conveys 'fuck it' so I leave, vanity stroked for the first time in months, apathetic about seeing the man but pleased that something unplanned has managed to penetrate the day.

2.

We have been exchanging emails. The man is an artist. I cannot remember what he looks like except that he is taller and older and unremarkable, although I have not seen anything remarkable for weeks now and doubt my ability to recognize its occurrence. The absolutes of the beauties I knew have been abdicating one by one, succeeded by aimless democratic greys.

The country gets colder and darker and quieter; I wait too eagerly for letters from friends to punctuate the week. I am weighing all of my food and not sleeping. In third person I experience myself replying to the ignored emails in the hope of enabling something that will take time out of a day, unable to quantify my actions in a chain of events that could bring about hurt or harm or significance of any kind. Time has become a restless ghost that I have to placate until it is time to escape its haunting. This man could be a deadline or a journey or a group of friends but unfortunately he is a man, unaware that I am going to use him to offset a temporal anxiety.

We arrange to meet for coffee on a Saturday morning, which is a different variety of morning for him and one like every other for me. He offers to pick me up in his car and I tell him that I will cycle. The ground is iced over and my wheel struggles to grip it, but I'm thankful for the austere brightness that mirrors light into the sky. A white path draws me downhill to the harbour and I see my red bike from above: a scalpel making a shallow, deliberate incision in the snow.

We are walking quickly, nervously, around the smaller of two lakes. He is all thick black wool and gives off an impression of being airtight. We discuss running, the English language and St Petersburg, where he studied. I tell him I lived with a girl from St Petersburg for two years and he seems unimpressed. I am further convinced that this is not a fact I should keep hauling out for every Russian person I meet, but I do this to keep myself from talking about three things:

Romantic ideas about Russia, which include gushing over the alphabet, Nabokov, and the golden era of the Trans-Siberian Railway.

Pussy Riot.

The time I nearly had a threesome with two Russian guys.

We enter the only decent cafe in town and I am a mute shadow, feeling unable to act responsibly or as something resembling myself. Usually I would press ahead first to make sure there is no question of him paying, but my lips are sullenly folded in on each other. He insists I choose a cake, and I look at the large glass lit up with kaleidoscopic confection, the sugar display being the locality's sole vibrancy. My receptors flare and I shake my head again in quiet terror, trying to smile. He selects a large slice of apple and almond tart which he motions we will share. He first joins me in selecting a cappuccino but then switches to a latte at the last moment. This seems weak.

He speaks mainly about himself and the 'North to South' series of paintings he is producing. He sometimes collaborates with his father, also a painter. I have taken to nodding and trying to draw out the lifespan of my coffee, which has been made in a teacup. Discovering that I too am an artist he immediately asks what I paint. I feel a deep part of myself give up. I had hoped for a degree of intellectual sparring or some momentary vehicle of escape but I am feeling restless and bored in his presence. I am the people strolling outside the window, looking in on a man earnestly telling a young woman about *verre églomisé*, and her carefully inspecting the tiny prisms on the back of her hands, to ensure they are still hers. My resentfulness triangulates myself: his bad knitwear, and the distinct lack of sexual tension.

He takes large, rough forkfuls of the frangipane and eats and talks without seeming to distinguish the two. He keeps jabbing the fork handle at me, urging me to take it. I finish my drink.

I thank him for the coffee and tell him I must go to the library, a fact he seems excited by. He tells me he has a meal with his volleyball team at seven but could we meet after? Zombie me nods and we arrange for him to pick me up from the town centre at ten. I sleepwalk back to my subterranean room and feel divorced from former selves.

Half an hour of googling his work reveals that his paintings are as uneventful as the morning has been.

3.

The day is a drop of oil in water, refusing to perforate. I cannot penetrate it or press my cheek to the enveloping tidal. I email the man and ask if he has a pair of Nordic walking poles, as I need photographs of them for a project. He says he will ask if he can borrow a friend's. I am now justifying the tryst in terms of its potential productive output.

How many favours can you ask of the universe?

Earlier in the year I lost my purse on the way to another country. The day before traveling I had stolen a single pair of black stockings from Marks & Spencer. The journey turned into a delirious guilt pilgrimage of trying to reconcile myself to leftover notions of the celestial: *I will be good I will be good I will be good.*

Amongst a sprawl of spontaneous notes on my desktop is the line 'FUCK TO PUNISH EXISTENCE'.

I hear the monotone of you telling me 'morality is a construct' and I know you would not approve of my interacting with this man, this anonymous card I have lifted up against the day. I listlessly apologize to you, myself, and my invisible but omnipresent heroines.

The meshes of the afternoon tighten. Outside, men sing songs of themselves. I breathe in until evening.

I step into the car and am overcome with a sickly wave of the parental, of one of the maybe three car journeys I have taken with my father. The passenger seat is on the wrong side and I have the surreal notion of being the adult in the driver seat, maybe taking him to or from a medical appointment; the accouterments of real life littering the dashboard. I am surprised by the age of the hand on the gearstick and try to imagine it placed on my flesh. I shudder and the two images layer but fail to merge.

'I got the poles,' he says, gesturing to the backseat excitedly.

I smile in reply and let the silence unravel, calmly relinquishing the idea of conversation. I had thought that the placing of my body on a different trajectory, maybe even in danger, would prompt a return to my immediacy with it; but the estrangement is more potent than ever. I wiggle my toes in my boots. My skin is akin to Disneyland.

I memorize the route for future reference, I'm a sensible adventurer after all and I need to find my way back in the snow. I won't be staying the night. We pass the motorway encircling the city and descend from its crest into grim suburbia. The car pulls up outside a block of flats with swings outside and I try to suppress a girlish, cinematic disappointment. It calls to mind the architecture of former encounters: vacuous bohemian promises of boys with mattresses on floors and sloping loft ceilings.

The material breakdown of the tiny flat is maybe 60% canvases, paints, easels and 40% clothes, hair bands and stationery of a solitary but loved, nine year-old girl. He steps over the threshold and gleefully holds up a hat with a cat's face on it, smiling at me.

'Don't worry, she is at a friend's house tonight. I am separated.'

My stomach folds over.

The small, sentient fraction of my brain clamours for the exit but I am unable to move, and I have come this far. All that's waiting for me at home is the basement room with geometries of cold laminate floor, the warmth of someone's home mocking me from above.

There is confusion when he thinks I want to eat and begins to cook pasta, and I mention I have eaten. He is nervous, unsure where to place me in his home, amongst his every day. He looks around worriedly for a seat and clears some paper from a red velour two-seater. I feel sorry for him but the pity is not enough to make me soothe his awkward advances; a feat so easily performed. I watch him calmly, silently.

In a panic he turns on the computer and begins to scroll through slideshows of work on his website (underestimating my capacity to google). I filter and murmur and nod at intervals. Some of the pieces are very beautiful; I am sure there was a time when they would have stirred me. He asks if I would like a drink and I follow him to the kitchen. There is champagne and a gelatinous strawberry-flavoured spirit, which, after looking agitatedly into the cupboard and muttering something about the dishwasher, he pours into two non-matching double shot glasses. I toast in Russian and we sip. It has the consistency and taste of Calpol. He tells me excitedly he buys it at duty free and looks like a child with its favourite sweets.

I return to the velour seat and he reappears a few minutes later with a plate of grapes and sliced persimmon. He places them tentatively next to me,

'You don't like cake, so.'

I am genuinely touched.

The conversation is staccato and he gentle; he makes no advances and I feel faint, not present, nodding at his words but anxiously tabulating the sugar content of the drink and the fruit I am unable to stop eating. I am willing him to take control of time and presence and the conversation; willing him to force me into some narrative that is out of my control; willing him to actualize the passivity that has crippled me since moving to this country. Instead he stumbles over his words, seemingly unprepared for my presence in his living room, offering me shy kindnesses.

I ask if we can take some photos with the poles and go to change into a sheer black dress I brought in my bag. I half undress in the cramped bathroom amongst his daughter's novelty flannels and shower gels. In the mirror I avoid my own eye contact and some interior vocality pulsates: *I am evil I am evil I am evil.*

'Wow,' he says, when I return. I am too sickened by myself to feel complimented. We move the velour seat away from the wall to clear space and use his camera as it is better than mine.

He takes photos of me and I see them but fail to recognize myself, amazed by the lens's inability to capture the reality of my fetid interior state. I watch as he attaches the folder to me in an email. He is a teacher helping me out with a school project. I am a child frustrated by the smallness of her hands and the bigness of the world.

His eyes are sad and old and I wonder if he feels used. I try to convey apology with my gaze and tell him that I should leave. He offers to drive me back and when I insist on walking he puts his coat on, too. Our paths dissect the snow by the swings and he is optimistic, listing places around the city and the country we could visit together, places hard to get to without a car, places that might remedy the heavy static and inertia that stultify life in the town. He is sweet, and in such an empty place I am perhaps his first foray into ideating escape in the form of another. The depressive pixie dream girl. Maybe we have used each other.

I think about his daughter, sleeping over at a friend's house, bickering about hair accessories and whispering to each other in the sacred corridor between the top and bottom bunk. I am more her than myself and the catch in my throat feels lunar.

At the crest overlooking the city I stop and repeat a female mantra: *thank you, goodbye, I know my way from here.* The path to the harbour is well lit. His smile is naive and he tells me that he will be in touch, that I must tell him when I am free. He looks genuinely happy about the course of the evening and he probably is; my hyperawareness does not speak for the universe. We kiss on the cheek and I turn to follow the lights, thick snow silencing my retreat. My face parts and the two halves flake and fall to the ground. My mind is raw to the night.

DAUGHTER, GOD DAUGHTER

Chrissie Gittins

Husk

I pulled up in the car park in front of Springbank House nursing home. Sunday was *the* day for visiting. All the cars, marshalled into neat rows, were bigger than mine. It was a sacred Sunday in December; the sky was clear, the light as strong and penetrating as it could be so near to the solstice.

Alice and I looked at one another. Alice's complexion was always pale, but now her skin was like milk which had lost its cream.

'Can I give you some cake?' said Alice.

'Yes, please.' She handed me a portion of poppy seed cake wrapped in foil, sent down by her sister from Leeds.

'I don't know how long I'll be,' Alice said.

'Don't worry. Be as long as you like.'

'How about if I meet you here at three, and let you know how it's going?' It was one o'clock by then.

'That's fine,' I said.

'Do you want to come in and I'll show you where you can

make a cup of tea?'

'That would be good. I'm desperate for the loo as well.'

'Sure. And I'll tell the staff who you are.' I nodded.

'Thanks for doing this,' said Alice. The trains were erratic that day, and she very much wanted to visit her mother again before beginning another working week. Her visit earlier in the week had been distressing – both for her and her mother. Alice wanted a different atmosphere to lie over the room where her mother lay on a rippling mattress, surrounded by spindle berries from her cherished garden. So I'd picked Alice up at Clapham South and we'd driven down to Esher.

I'd known Alice's mother, Merryn, for almost as long as I'd known Alice. Twenty-five years. Alice and I met on our first day at art college. Alice had a flask of coffee and I had a stack of sandwiches; we pooled our resources. At first I visited Alice's parents *with* Alice; then, after Merryn's husband died, I visited on my own.

We'd have lunch, weed and lop together, then drop accumulated cuttings off at the council tip. We'd have tea in the living room, with extra hot water on standby from the kettle beside Merryn's winged armchair. There'd be extended conversations over iced coffee biscuits, fruitcake and shortbread. There was a day in March we went on an outing. We had Wisley gardens almost to ourselves. Merryn scrambled through the mud and rain to scrutinize any plant that caught her eye. We both stood mesmerized by a bank dotted with yellow hoop petticoat narcissus. When a rat moved into my flat and ate my soap, Merryn sent a selection of fragrant new soaps. When my car crashed, she sent Garrison Keillor.

'I feel embarrassed that you're not going to see her,' said Alice as we approached the A3. Now that Merryn was dying she wanted only closest family to visit.

'That's alright. I wouldn't want it any other way.' I was glad to be able to help. Since Alice had told me of Merryn's brain tumour three months before, I had slipped into a treacly chasm.

The nursing home was a triple-fronted substantial Victorian

house, with just enough charm to make it attractive. There was a hanging basket beside the front door. Alice peered into it. 'The pansies have revived. They were limp when I came on Tuesday. Frosted.'

Alice remembered the code to open the front door and whispered it in my ear.

The warmth of the house was welcome, but not oppressive. There was a display of silk flowers on the hall table, and a notice board with photographs of residents blowing out birthday candles and opening presents. The Christmas decorations were thankfully minimal and subtle. Alice showed me the kitchen, the kettle, the cupboard with mugs, and the jars of instant coffee and dusty teabags.

As we climbed the stairs I noticed the framed prints staggered up the wall – wheelbarrows, ancient farm equipment, botanical illustrations. Alice pointed to the toilet at the end of the landing.

'Just tell me where your Mum is,' I asked. I knew she was near, and needed to place her in this warren of doors and corridors.

'She's at the end of that landing, on the left.' Alice pointed in the opposite direction, then kissed me on both cheeks. She managed a smile as she walked away.

Every door carried the name of the person inside. 'Doris Precious' was behind the door next to the toilet. On each door handle hung a hand-stitched toy – a long limbed monkey, a ballerina, a billowing clown. I wasn't sure if they were part of the Christmas decorations or permanent fixtures. Were they supposed to remind the staff before they entered the room that each resident had once been a child? Were they there to help the residents feel they were individuals, and not merely part of an institution?

I knew something of what was inside Merryn's room from what Alice had told me. Above her bed was the shield of Cornwall, her home county – a triangle of golden coins on a black background. Beside her bed were three books – 'Alice in

Wonderland' with Tenniel's drawings, 'A Midsummer Night's Dream' and 'The Merchant of Venice'. Merryn had asked Alice to read to her from 'Alice in Wonderland' – from the chapter which begins with the playing-card-gardeners painting a white rose tree red. There was also a pinboard displaying all the cards she had received, including the ones from me – a Zuberon still life with cup and rose, a serene Morandi, an early jewelled Rothko, and Leonardo's pencil studies of violets and cherry blossom. Merryn, who had lived all her life without a television, now requested DVD's – 'Blythe Spirit' and 'The Hound of the Baskervilles'. And finally, 'Henry V'.

At first Merryn replied to my cards, her always-welcome handwriting only a little shaky. On the first envelope she remembered all of my address apart from the house number. On the second there were three kisses by my name, and the address had been added by someone else. The final two envelopes were addressed by Alice.

I struggled to know what to say when I wrote the cards. At first I caught her up with my projects, reported back on the nasturtiums and nicotania sylvestris still flowering in my garden. But as I inched slowly towards accepting that Merryn was going to die, I realized I had to say what was in my heart.

'You've always been such a lovely friend, darling,' said Merryn in her first card – the Cutty Sark racing home for the Royal National Lifeboat Institution. She had written 'Ship Ahoy!' beside her greeting. In her second her mind must have been ranging over her life; she'd been thinking of the Gregorian chant books she'd seen in Italy with her husband, and of large floppy butterflies being poked by birds. She'd ordered bulbs for a special 'Spring Display' at her home she'd left in Esher. Her third card commented on my Leonardo card – how he must have drawn the violets and cherry blossom straight away, as they were so obviously fresh.

In Merryn's final card, Alice now her amanuensis, she said how much she appreciated the cards, but really I mustn't feel the need to send many more because she knew how much I had to do, and the important thing was that I had time for my writing and painting. I took this last consideration as rejection. My skin was so thin at that time it could not protect me, not even from the glance of a feather.

I let myself out of Springbank House, the door clicking behind me. Alice had pointed out a side road that led to a path across some fields. The gardens of the compact cottages along the road were straddled with the skeletons of summer – hollyhock stalks with bulging seed heads, the blots of rudbekias, plates of sedums and alchemilla. The path rose up and over a bridge then ran alongside a field of caramel cows. I could see puddles in the depressions in the path, sealed with thin sheets of ice. When I gently pressed my foot on the ice lids, bubbles jostled beneath the surface.

I thought about the house that Merryn had left behind; the sight of the 1930's gable which heralded every visit, mauve candy tuft by the front door, pink amaryllis strengthening under the bay, a jasmine hedge to inhale on arrival. My eyes would rove as I made for the front door's throaty bell and Merryn's warm welcome; purple morning glory climbing the fence, the leaves of cyclamen nestling in the beds, a lavender bush making its presence felt beside the path. How must it have been for her to think of leaving all this behind? The carved oak writing desk in the front room where she pursued her correspondence with bishops and prime ministers; the dining table in the back room where so many celebratory meals had been eaten with family and friends; the glass-covered bookshelves in both rooms holding Milton, Donne, Clare, Marvell.

Alice said that since being admitted to Springbank House Merryn hadn't mentioned her home, apart from indicating precisely where in the back garden the bulbs she had ordered should be planted. This made Alice think that managing it had become too much for her. But at some point, at many points, Merryn must have thought about how it would be to leave her home.

A cyclist came up behind me, rode through a collection of

puddles and crunched the ice into jagged pieces. The lemon light was low and the sun no longer visible. I turned back and retraced my steps.

In the car I listened to the radio and ate the poppy seed cake. By three o'clock every window was steamed up. I saw Alice appear at the front door, she scanned the carpark for my silver-blue Peugeot. I switched on the windscreen wipers and waved out of the window. Alice waved back, ran over, and eased herself into the passenger seat.

'I couldn't find you. I thought your car was red. So much for visual acuity.'

'Almost right. My last car was red. How is she?'

Alice sighed. 'She's like a husk.'

'Oh, love.'

'She says she's content. She can't say she's happy, but she's content.'

'Could she chat?'

'She told me she loves me.'

Indian Soap

I parked my car on a side street off the South Circular and slammed the door particularly hard. I resented having to come here every Wednesday night for eight o'clock. Though it *was* my choice. Or was it? I didn't see myself as having a choice. Before the first appointment I'd been so apprehensive I had to tackle my geraniums to keep control of myself. I took them down from their shelf – pink, pinker, white and pink – and one by one stripped them of their dead leaves.

It was a dark dank night; not cold enough to be invigorating, and not warm enough to dry the pavements of rain. I pressed the bell of the Garret Centre. The timing had to be exactly right. The therapists had to have ended their previous session in order to be able to answer the door. It might be my own therapist who answered, more often than not it wasn't.

I sat in the waiting room, waiting to be called. The occupants barely acknowledged each other, despite their proximity. I watched the minutes tick away, wondering what we would talk about. At this stage it never seemed to me that there was anything *to* talk about.

Sylvia appeared. I followed her up the stairs. I resented Sylvia's black leather boots, her silk pleated skirt, her glossy blonde hair. I couldn't remember when I'd last taken an interest in my appearance – I picked up the same clothes day after day. Sylvia was slight and graceful, I felt heavy and leaden. I walked through the door of her room, took off my coat and sat in the chair next to the window and the radiator. The thin navy curtains were not quite closed, but I could see the streetlights through the gap. I wouldn't look out of the window again till the end of the session.

Sylvia always waited for me to speak first.

'Merryn died at the weekend.'

'How did you find out?'

'Alice phoned me.' I paused. 'But I think I already knew. Merryn sent me some soap. A selection. There was an emerald green one, from India. Aromatic. Wonderful. On Saturday I cleaned the bathroom – there were just two small pieces left on the sink. When I looked again the pieces had formed themselves into a heart shape.' I paused again. 'I didn't get upset. My heart was heavy. But I think I've grieved already.'

'You'd been doing a lot of grieving. And it must be very difficult for you because you're a friend of the family, not a family member. You must feel as though you are very much on the outside.'

I didn't feel this, and I was surprised by what she said, but I didn't contradict her.

'Alice has asked me to read 'The Wren' by John Clare at the funeral.'

A double decker bus accelerated on the road outside.

'I stopped sleeping when Merryn was first diagnosed. I was asked by two different doctors within forty-eight hours if I intended to take my own life.'

'That must have been frightening.'

'I was already frightened… I don't understand why I can't sleep.'

'Are you still taking medication?'

'Sleeping tablets and anti-depressants. The sleeping tablets give me four hours a night then I wake up.'

'The feelings you are having are too painful to allow you to sleep.' This sounded too glib an explanation to me, but I did like its simplicity. I looked at the clock, which stood on a filing cabinet to the left of Sylvia. Sylvia glanced at the clock above my head.

'Do you think I should do my school bookings next week?'

'How many days is it?'

'Three. Two nights away from home. In Cumbria.'

'I think it's time to re-connect with that part of yourself. Your career is very important to you.'

'The alternative is very bleak. To not do them. But everything feels such hard work.'

There was a pause.

'A friend phoned me yesterday morning. I was concentrating on just trying to feel normal. I only told her last week how I am. She knows about my Mum – her manic depression, or bi-polar or whatever you call it… It took me a long time to tell her.'

'Because of the shame you felt?' Sylvie crossed her legs.

'I suppose so.'

'She said, 'Did your father suffer from depression?' She's driving along in her car and she asks me a question like that! It knocked me right back. I'm trying to talk about what's happening to me so people get an idea of what it's like. But saying something like that – she's *no* idea. *And* she's suffered from depression herself.'

There was another pause. Sylvie held my gaze.

'Another friend suggested I become a volunteer at the Dulwich Picture Gallery. I can't volunteer in my own life, let alone the Dulwich Picture Gallery. People don't know what you need. Most people.'

'What do you need?'

'For people just to be there. To listen. Not to leave me alone.'

'It's good that you are trying to explain. And I have to say you are working very hard in these sessions, and between the sessions.'

I looked at the spider plants cascading down the table behind Sylvia.

'When Merryn adopted me as her god-daughter at her husband's funeral she asked me to go down and help her with the garden. We'd talk and talk and talk. She was interested in everything.'

'I think one of the reasons you have felt the loss so deeply is that you could be a child with Merryn. You talk about chatting and having tea… You didn't have any responsibility for her. These are very old feelings we are dealing with. You couldn't be a child with your own mother – you had too much responsibility.'

'It wasn't her fault,' I said fiercely.

Lemon Chiffon

As we left the house to attend the funeral Alice said goodbye to her mother once more. Goodbye to her bent fingers, which arranged gentians and sweet peas in delicate vases for the dining table, goodbye to her soft cheek which she pressed against Alice's in greeting, goodbye to her trickling voice which stroked Alice's wounds and sang at her every triumph.

'Are you alright carrying that?' I asked Alice as we went out of the front door. I had driven down from London to Esher with two massive lemon chiffon cakes which Alice had ordered the week before. 'Three layers of citrus sponge filled and iced with tangy lemon frosting, made with organic unwaxed lemons. The perfect celebration cake,' said the Konditor and Cook website.

'I'm fine. How about you, Kitty?' asked Alice looking behind her. Kitty was Alice's older sister. She was clasping the other cake close to her chest.

'It *is* heavy but I'm sure I'll manage,' said Kitty.

'We can take it in turns,' I said.

'I've got two strong arms,' said Rosemary, clenching her fists.

It was three years since I had buried my own mother. I'd kept all her silver toast racks. In my studio in New Cross I was making pencil drawings of each one. The walls were lined with evocations – shiny ribbed bars welded to looped handles.

The four of us assembled on the pavement.

'How long will it take to get to the church hall?' I asked.

'About twenty minutes,' said Alice.

'I just needed to know.'

'Of course.'

Alice looked back at the house. The winter flowering jasmine was shooting its yellow flowers around the front door, two stone pots stood on either side smug with the promise of Queen of the Night tulips. I went to stand beside Alice. She leaned her head on my shoulder until she was ready to go.

We wound around the suburban streets, passing ample semis with mature gardens. As we approached the traffic lights on the main road Alice rested her cake on a garden wall.

'Shall I take over?' I asked.

'Yes, please,' said Alice. 'I don't think I've got much upper arm strength.'

'I'm not sure I've got much more,' I said.

'Can I take yours?' said Rosemary to Kitty.

'I'd like that. Shall I carry your bag?' Kitty placed the white box on Rosemary's outstretched arms and Rosemary wrapped her gloved hands around it.

'How are Peter and Sarah?' I asked Kitty.

'Oh, they're fine. Peter will probably be knocking seven bells out of a football, and Sarah... putting whale stickers on her exercise books. Something like that.'

Kitty lived two hundred miles from her mother's house. In recent months when she was looking after her children she thought she should be looking after her mother. When she was looking after her mother she thought she should be with her children. Her mother's death had ended that particular dilemma. But now, when she was back in Leeds, she inhabited every room of her mother's house. She saw Merryn sifting her fingers through the buds of lavender that she'd rubbed into Chinese porcelain bowls. She heard the rattling of silver cutlery as Merryn replaced it in the felt-lined drawer. She saw her gazing at the arching leaves of five amaryllis stored in the back bedroom as they waited to bloom downstairs.

'Not far to go now,' said Alice encouragingly as we rounded the last corner.

Rosemary lived five thousand miles from *her* mother. She'd left her behind in Zimbabwe. They spoke on the phone occasionally and Rosemary sent her money regularly. Merryn had greeted Rosemary when she first saw her, as she did everyone she met in her road. Rosemary asked if she knew anyone who needed a cleaner. Merryn had been meaning to get help, so Rosemary began to clean for her. As Merryn became more frail she took increasing care of her. They both said an angel had brought them together.

By the time we arrived at the church hall we'd all carried each cake once. The verdict was that one cake was heavier than the other. We dropped them off at the village hall and made our way to the church opposite. Alice pointed out the English flag flying over the church steeple at half-mast. Not many parishioners were given this honour. The verger met us at the doorway wearing a red fleece. 'I must apologize,' she said, 'I'm not properly dressed yet. It's just so cold.' The church was already filling up.

The vicar told of Merryn and the man she married. How he was a friend of her brother's at Cambridge, and due to visit their Cornish home during the summer holidays for the second year running. Merryn mounted her bicycle and pedalled into St Austell. She came back carrying three new dresses. 'I had nothing to wear,' she told her family. They realised then there was something brewing. Within six months they were married.

When the service was over, the seventy or so congregation funnelled into the church hall. Vases of early narcissus and sprays of leaves from Merryn's garden had been placed at intervals around the windowsills and on the stage. A table held a selection of colour and black and white photographs of Merryn, from when she was a toddler, to a sunny lunch on a recent holiday in Greece. The two yellow moon-cakes stood on a table opposite, at the end of lines of teacups and sherry glasses. The words on the top of each cake – 'Merryn, with love' – were piped in red icing between hearts and stars.

Kitty and Alice went from group to group thanking their friends and relatives for coming. A man approached them for details of their family, so that he could make a page on the church website about the funeral. A woman approached Alice to ask for Rosemary's details, so that she could offer her some cleaning work.

Rosemary and I sat together at a table near the cakes with a plate of food each from the buffet.

'I'm going to measure those cakes and see if one *is* bigger than the other,' I said.

I used my fork to measure their diameters, flipping it over till I reached the far side of each cake.

'I'm right. This one is nearly a third of a fork bigger!'

Rosemary laughed and I sat down again.

'How do you find living in Esher?' I asked.

'Some people are nice, some aren't. Last week I got told to go back to Brixton.'

'Oh dear.'

'My local church isn't very friendly. I go to Croydon to pray.'

'That's rather a long way.'

'I came here to live with my sister. She's a nurse. But she moved to America.'

Just then the caterer thought she should cut the cakes and have them ready for anyone who wanted to eat something sweet. She took a large knife from the kitchen and began to slice the first cake. I scraped back my chair and darted over to Alice.

'Letting you know that the cakes are now being cut. Not sure if that's what you wanted,' I said quietly.

'Thank you,' said Alice. She got to the cake table as the second slice was being cut.

'Do you mind if *I* cut the cakes?' she asked.

'No, not at all.' The caterer handed her the knife.

Alice pointed the knife into the centre of the cake and felt the resistance of the dense sponge as she pressed gently downwards. She tipped the slice over onto its side and slid the knife underneath before slithering it onto a waiting plate. The guests began to gather round. Alice sliced the rest of the cake and handed out each plate with a smile and a serviette. Then she set about the second cake.

CEUM NA CAILLICH

Neil Campbell

They left the camper van in the car park at North Sannox Bridge, intent on a horseshoe walk that would take them up Sail an Im and Castail Abhail and back down past Suidhe Fhearghas. Following the Sannox Burn along a distinct path they looked at the glistening and shining waterfalls that ran down past them and collected in deep pools.

Emerging through a pine plantation they looked up to see the skyline and the dress circle ridge along which Simon had planned they would walk; a dress circle ridge leading to Ceum na Caillich. They crossed the burn higher up and began a tough ascent through cotton grass and bracken and heather. The path, distinct on the other side of the burn, eroded now into a loop of hard stones before fading into a flattening of the cotton grass. White butterflies flew around them.

Libby stopped, breathing heavily, disheartened, her heart never having been in the walk in the first place. He had always walked. She knew it. And she knew that she had to show some enthusiasm. He'd taken her to all the places he'd walked before.

They'd never gone anywhere new. She'd always said to

him how she wanted to go to the west of Ireland and meet her relatives there. But they always went back to his beloved Scotland and she realized she'd come to hate it.

'Come on,' said Simon, brushing away a dragonfly. 'You'll have it dark. You wanted to do these kinds of walks so come on, let's get on with it. It'll be easier once we get up there.'

'I just need to sit down for a minute' she said, easing herself down onto a slanted rock. Simon stood above her, smilingly competitive, gazing up at the ridge in the sky he knew to be the promontory of stunning views.

When Libby stood up, Simon at once began marching off ahead of her again, following the contours of the land now that the path seemed to have vanished, bearing right and then swinging left to make a more gradual ascent of Sail an Im. He loved how these mountain trails always seemed to take the most intelligent course, the routes of crofters before the clearances. When he was inexperienced he had always made short cuts, taking straight lines for the summit, making his ascents much quicker and considerably more arduous. By now he'd mellowed a little, and when he remembered he made a conscious choice to slow down, to enjoy being on the mountain, to look around at the broadening vista or closer at the shifting white of the cotton grass. But he didn't look back to see where Libby was and she cursed him out of earshot.

Ceum na Caillich was still there, the profile in granite above them. Translated from the Gaelic as 'the witche's step' it was clear how it got its name. Where the ridge rolled along gently across the summit of Castail Abhail in a series of benevolent tors, at the notorious step the summit slipped starkly downwards, cutting a slanted and treacherous V into the mountain.

Libby was too tired to have realized their prospective route, and Simon hadn't told her. He remembered when he'd done this walk previously, the fear he'd felt that first time so many years before, on his own, when the sun had been blazing, the day he'd been ravaged by horseflies. He'd stayed at Lochranza and done a walk around the headland to a deserted white cottage.

There he'd sat down in hot sunshine and looked out at the haze above the Firth of Clyde. The water blurred with the sky. A seal was basking on a rock and the coastline was completely silent. The ghostly reflections of white yachts floated motionlessly on the flat water. A man in a kayak passed as though slowly flying. And time and again Simon was bitten by horseflies.

It was these memories that made Simon doubt himself below Ceum na Caillich. He thought it a sly joke that experience had made him feel more vulnerable rather than more confident. He had sprung down the descent without problems that last time. The weather had been sunny then. He was older now and Libby was older than he was. He was surprised by the way he was sweating and breathing heavily, even at the summit of Sail an Im.

As they sat apart, Simon gulping their water, Libby took in the view down towards the sea loch at Lochranza. Grey clouds blew in as Libby remembered when they'd stayed there, and how there were no facilities except a little sandwich shop and a butcher, and how she missed the Co-op they had in Lamlash. She remembered how, on a bright sunny day, they'd walked along the road to the tiny ferry port at Claonaig and how she wanted to take a day trip to Kintyre, maybe carry on to Jura.

As she nibbled on her oatcakes, high up on Sail an Im, Libby could see the tiny ferry crossing the dark waters of Kilbrannan Sound. On that day previously, Simon had insisted they go back to the Lochranza Hotel, and with the hot sun and the views outside they sat in the little lounge bar. Simon had ordered white bait for them. Libby left half of it and sat there in the shaded surrounds, thinking of the ferry crossing to Claonaig, and the sun outside, and the ruins of Lochranza Castle, and how it seemed they always did what Simon wanted them to do. In the corrie below Sail an Im, groups of red deer, some half hidden by bracken, looked directly across at them, ears raised, before moving away and looking back again. One of them made a gentle grunt in their direction.

The distance of the walk was just over six miles, with three thousand feet of total ascent. And it was at Sail an Im that it would have been wise for Simon and Libby to turn back. With dark clouds gathering, they were already too tired. But after a short rest they continued a little further upwards and the route flattened out to a clearly marked ridge walk. For Simon these ridges were the best kind of walking. The high ground reached, he was able to stroll and look around for ravens and eagles. Libby welcomed the respite too, for a forgotten moment even seeming to enjoy the adventure of it, an adventure she didn't know the half of yet. In the silences of the summit walk Libby heard the beguiling croak of a couple of ravens high overhead. It wasn't their loud calling, it was a gentle communication between the two birds, and it sounded intimate, as though they held the privacy of the entire sky.

Simon and Libby put on their jackets in preparation for what seemed the inevitable rain, and when it came it lashed them in a rushing wind, a rushing wind Simon hoped would mean the rain passed over them quickly. But it didn't. As the rain came the wind dropped again, and a view he'd been expecting of Cir Mhor and Beinn Tarsuinn was lost to the black pause of the clouds. The granite tors around them slickened in the wet and Simon abandoned any plan to climb to the summit of Castail Abhail. Now was the time to keep as close to the path as they could. And still they had yet to reach Ceum na Caillich. Simon noticed the path leading off towards Cir Mhor, the one that later led gently down into Glen Rosa, but the camper van was back at North Sannox Bridge, and there was no avoiding Ceum na Caillich.

When they reached the jagged descent Simon instructed Libby to follow his exact route. She looked down into the chasm and couldn't believe he'd take her on a walk as dangerous as this, worse that he wouldn't tell her about it first. It was typical of his selfishness. She couldn't go all the way back. In her fatigue she almost didn't care if she fell. She had been stumbling from tiredness across the edges of the easy ridge path, and she watched as Simon inched his way down, his hands grabbing the granite before he sat on his backside, seemingly about to slide. She watched his progress from above and looked beyond him to the gully where she'd be safe. His legs were fatigued, and when his heel slipped he didn't have the strength to recover his balance. His hands reached at rain as he fell down. His head glanced off a granite outcrop. Then he seemed to stop a moment before he started falling more rapidly. He shouted as he fell and the shout was cut short by his landing. In the silence broken only by the rain falling on Ceum na Caillich, Libby heard him landing in the gully some thirty feet below her.

She stopped still for a moment, her heart racing, and immediately saw how he should have descended; there was a thin trail between rocks that clearly showed a safer way. She gripped the wet granite in her hands as she went down, hugged it in parts so that the sharp rock ripped at her jacket and ragged at the cuticles of her fingers.

In the gully she grabbed wet granite and steadied her shaking legs, took a deep breath and then walked over to Simon. His head was covered in blood and he was unconscious. She took off her coat and covered his crumpled body. She searched the numbers in her mobile and tried calling mountain rescue but there was no reception. She reached into Simon's pockets for the keys to the camper van and then covered him again with her coat. She could see through the rain towards a path off to the left leading down the gully, and then a path leading off from that to the right, around the base of Ceum na Caillich. She checked the mobile but still there was no reception.

Libby followed the clear path along to Suidhe Fhearghas. There was a ray of sunlight through the shifting clouds and for a moment the granite on the footpath sparkled. Libby looked across to the grey immensity of the Sound of Bute that seemed joined to the grey waves of cloud in the sky. There was a tiny white yacht all alone out there.

Libby kept descending towards Sannox on a very steep path that disappeared into heather and thistle and bracken and thorns, all the time stopping to check her phone. Finally she saw the white camper van, tiny in the parking area at North

Sannox Bridge. There were no other cars and she looked at her mobile phone again. Still there was no reception. Shivering with adrenaline and cold she continued towards the van.

Few cars passed along the long tarmac road that ran down the hill from above Lochranza and down into Sannox. Libby struggled through a group of trees near the valley floor and heard a raven in the rain. She struggled lower and lower, continually slipping onto her backside, before she ploughed through a stretch of heather and slicked bracken and thorns and finally stepped onto the tarmac.

As Libby sat in the camper van she started to scratch at her hands, her neck and the small of her back. Then she started to scratch at her face. She looked back into the van with its kitchen unit and the little fridge, and the couch that folded out into a bed, and there were midges everywhere. She looked at the phone and still there was no reception.

With all the windows open and the heater blasting, she started the camper van and pulled out of the parking area at North Sannox Bridge heading south. She reached the Sannox Hotel and called the mountain rescue from the landline in the lobby. They told her to stay where she was. She watched through the rain lashed windows as the waves washed ashore at Sannox Bay. A little old lady offered tea to calm her nerves. She drank it, was warmed by the gesture and the liquid even as she burned her tongue. The rain crashed against the windows. Libby looked at the sky, heard the rumble. She ran outside into the rain and looked up and saw the yellow mountain rescue helicopter disappearing and reappearing among the clouds. She waved at it, pointed stupidly toward the hills. Cyclists passed in procession along the coastal road, oblivious to everything but the rain.

The old lady in the hotel was talking to a barmaid. When Libby looked towards them they looked away. The old lady came back with some cheese and told Libby to eat. Libby laughed at the sight of the cheese on the plate. She got back in the van and drove back to North Sannox Bridge. All the way back she tried to look up for the helicopter and more than once nearly knocked over a cyclist. She braked to a halt on the gravel of the car park and got out of the van. There were no cars on the road; just cyclists labouring up the hill. The rain had stopped but the Sannox Burn roared under the bridge. She was bitten on her hand by a mosquito and an orange bubble began to appear. She looked up towards Suidhe Fhearghas. A golden eagle floated above the ridgeline. Libby couldn't hear or see the helicopter. Still there was no reception on her phone. She stood in the car park at North Sannox Bridge as the roaring of the burn grew louder. There was an information board showing a map and detailing wildlife and flora and fauna. She kicked at it. She looked at the van. She'd left the driver's door open. The keys were still swinging from the ignition as ravens appeared in the sky.

She got back in the van. She passed through Sannox and reached the Corrie Hotel and the bunkhouse where they'd stayed on a previous visit. She looked at the picnic tables under the wet parasols that looked out across the Firth of Clyde, remembering another stupid argument there. She thought the scenic places of Scotland were just venues for their bickering. He didn't respect her; he had never respected her.

Driving on she saw the stone seal on a rock that fools everyone on their first visit. The seal that, even when the waves lash over it stays fixed in the same place, unlike the real seals that slip easily off their rocks as the tide comes in. Further out, she saw the approach of the Calmac Ferry, although the ferry itself didn't seem to be making any waves.

She took her hands off the wheel to scratch at them, swerving a little on the narrow coast road near Merkland Point. She scratched at her neck and face as she passed Brodick Castle, almost hitting a cyclist. She drove further around Brodick Bay to the car park at the ferry port. She went into the boarding area, showing her return ticket to a man in a little yellow cabin.

In the claustrophobic parking area in the hull of the boat she sat there as others pulled up beside and behind her.

She stayed still as the ferry started its crossing, sitting in the camper van he'd 'bought for them'. Getting out of the van and into the echoing hull of the ferry she climbed two flights of stairs. She looked at her phone and it had run out of charge. She had a coffee in the cafe and looked at the headlines in *The Arran Banner* before standing up to go outside. On deck she could smell the water. Sea spray flicked against her jacket. The helicopter passed through the sky above her and a white gull flew above the grey waves, getting knocked back by the wind.

KISS ON A THREAD

Matthew Temple

Grey men dance badly to disco tunes beneath a glitterball that hasn't been there for them for forty years and she appears, the scorched bitch he calls her now, *my dime-dollar plaything*, dress bold enough, short enough to shock pink. She crosses to a spot where mistletoe was hanging by a thread, another party, until all the kissing stopped and those poison white berries turned brown. His wife is first to see, a kick to her belly that isn't the child he never wanted until his choice was whittled down, fatherhood or fake remorse, exhausting charades for him, a man who hates children and loved every fuck with the woman under mistletoe, long gone. She stands, turns to him and everyone turns to her, family and friends, a loose-tongued crowd, they know who she is, they know. Slow and calm, a pulse of cleavage the only clue adrenaline, albeit iced tonight, is permitted in her veins, she rotates her arms behind her back, hands nest on lumbar arc, and shuts her eyes, mascara rustles. Now silence. Even the bubbles in rented flutes dare not make a sound, not a pop, as she pushes together her lips, beautiful terrible things, a face slashed by original sin you'd think to hear them talk, and there she waits for *his* kiss. She waits, she waits. Sickness hits the wife, harsh nausea not maternal, never that, and a white napkin, also rented, is her only support. He, the man, the husband, the father-to-be with no wish to be, is too busy hating to care. His lust is neutered by emotions he doesn't feel but must display to save something he may one day need, when his loins become a nuisance easy to ignore, by him and her and all the other hers in the world. Lust gone, hate remains yet she stands there, lips full pout, oblivious to the violence between his ears, he wants to throw her from a skyscraper ten million storeys tall, any city you name, and watch the sidewalk soak her up until the memory of his own fall is a stain rubbed away and washed away by strangers' feet and pissing dogs. Rub her away, he thinks. Piss her away, he thinks. But she stands there, eyes shut, same spot, until a boy in a readymade bow-tie, yellow and black, hair slicked with grandma's spit, walks up to the standing dame and lifts himself up on tiptoes, sandals creaking, and sets his small lips for another kiss that never comes.

BLUE

Roelof Bakker

You're on the Victoria line. Southbound towards Brixton. It's the morning rush hour. The carriage is packed. A tin of baked beans. You've claimed some standing room sandwiched in-between the sitting people hiding behind their handsets and free newspapers.

A pink-haired woman is reading *Place* by Jorie Graham. You're trying to decipher the small print. Lean forward a little. It says WINNER OF THE PULLITZER PRIZE. You don't know the book. You don't read poetry. You've heard of the prize though.

How many people can be packaged together into one carriage? You did a rough headcount once. You reckoned about two hundred human persons to the max (with room for bags, suitcases, buggies and the odd dog). All these strangers thrown together, up-close and impersonal – each keeping their distance. No speaking.

Your arms dangle on either side of your body. Your feet point in the direction of the moving train. Are placed slightly apart. Your right foot leads, with your left foot about twelve inches behind. This way you can easily manoeuvre your body during unexpected turbulence. It's as if you're on a skateboard, keeping your balance as the carriage speeds ahead.

You're freestanding. Holding on to nothing. You're not involved. You're not a part of it.

Other standing passengers cling on to the bright blue bars high above the seats. Shorter, standing passengers prefer the vertical bars painted a darker blue, like the blue in the Union Jack.

An unexpected jerk as the car breaks. You grab the bar above your head. You nearly miss it. You could have landed into a stranger's lap. You would have felt safe for one brief moment. Belonged.

The metal is cold. The chill has penetrated your fingers. The bar is sticky. Snot. Hand cream. Chicken fat. You're hanging on to someone else's filth.

*

You make your way up the stairs to the top of the tall, upright building with solid foundations. Like the kind of man you've been dreaming about. Tall, strong. Supportive, safe.

Twenty-one storeys, two hundred and seventy three steps. You count each aloud as you climb up to the top. You ascend slowly, holding on to the railing as if attending a ballet class, elegantly gripping the barre. But there's no mirror to watch your reflection and see how well you perform your fancy steps or newly acquired moves.

You race as fast as you can up to the next level. Your backpack jumps furiously up and down, your heart is speeding. The adrenalin rush of an army assault course.

The door to the roof is padlocked. You find the hammer in your backpack and use it to smash the lock. The piercing northern wind bites your face as you open the door. You walk across the roof. You stop when you reach the ledge. Over it is nothing. You stand behind it. The whole of London is there in front of your eyes. You breathe in minuscule fragments of everyone who has ever passed through this enormous city.

A gust of wind throws you backwards. Confirms your loneliness. There are no bars to grip. There's not a soul to latch on to. There is no support.

You lift your right foot and step onto the ledge. Your left foot follows. You can see the car park below. A tiny figure is unloading furniture from the back of a van.

You have that same urge as when you stood on the edge of the cliffs at Beachy Head last summer. A beckoning. A dare. An invitation to dance. But you feel neither dizzy nor scared this time. You've made up your mind.

Feet and legs pressed together. Shoulders square. Arms elongated at the sides of your body, slowly rising until at shoulder height. You look like the Angel of the North.

No clouds. The sky is blue.

KILLING WITH KINDNESS

Ailsa Cox

David looked like a Red Indian, with high cheekbones and a razor straight nose and a strip of hair running across his shaved head. You could see the shape of his skull under the bristles. I loved to stroke the sleek skin and bone and the chilly contours of his ears. He looked dead scary when you first met him, and just to wind you up he'd narrow his eyes sometimes and stare at you, and then his thin mouth would crinkle into a smile, a little boy smile, that changed his face completely. Some people wondered what I saw in David. I wondered what he saw in me.

The front door opens and gently shuts. The man with the briefcase slips from the house, almost invisible in the January morning. The car slides down the black streets, headlights blazing. Not a soul about. Not a soul. On the radio, the latest on the arctic whale stuck in the Thames. *Rescue attempts underway – vets on standby – an effort to turn its course back towards the open sea.* Not a soul about, no sign of life, not a cat or a mouse. Everyone's asleep.

I just don't get this. I can't work it out. I remember we were camped out on the dunes, drinking vodka and swallowing these little orange pills – I think they were orange? I said, 'I'm scared,' and David said, 'I'm with you.' Then everything went dark. Waking up, it was like coming round in hospital, except that this time I was all by myself. And I still am. I've not seen a soul. Feels like morning to me, early morning. The tide's so far out the sea merges with the sky and the hazy outlines of New Brighton. My hair's damp and sticky with salt, my body aching like when you've been sitting for hours in the back of the car. What happened to my shoes? And where's David? I'm calling his name as loud as I can but my voice gets lost in the wind.

Still dark when he stops to fill up with petrol, swigging on a Red Bull as he gets back in the car. This is the bleakest part of winter, when Christmas and New Year are done with, and spring far ahead – a time when he used to look forward to his birthday, in those days when was first taken into care. Now he can't even remember how old he is without reminding himself of the year and working backwards. But he's not in bad shape for close on forty-eight. Got most of his hair, and no paunch to speak of – for the simple reason that he hasn't touched a drink for thirty years.

The picture of the whale is splashed on all the papers, ploughing upstream past the Houses of Parliament – what's that expression the kids use? On a mission. And thinking about kids makes him think about his stepdaughter Lola. Which he has sworn not to do.

The first words David said to me were piss off. Run home to your mother. I said I haven't got a mother. She's dead. And he said I haven't got anything for you, but I knew that he had.

Then this girl came to the door, a blonde girl, squashy and lazy, her slow drifting eyes caked with liner and mascara. Go on then, David, ask your friend inside.' And then she disappeared back into the darkness.

The lock clicked as he shut the door behind him. We stood there together on the landing.

'Who told you to come here?'

'No one. Give me some speed.'

He seemed amused, the only word for it, amused. 'I don't know what you're talking about.'

'Everyone knows about you.'

'Oh do they?' He turned his back on me and then, realising he'd locked himself out, he leaned his head against the door and sort of groaned. 'Alright. Come and see me tomorrow – on the sands, first thing in the morning. Six o'clock.'

'*Six?*'

'That's what I said. Now fuck off.'

On a mission – not even knowing himself what force propels him down these murky byways. The whale has turned into a sign of redemption as men wade through the mud, baptising him with river water and shepherding his great hide out of the shallows. All that effort – the cranes and hoists and pontoons – moving into place. How good people are, how kind at heart, even those who have not yet surrendered themselves to the Lord's safekeeping. The city is momentarily suspended, taking its eyes off figures and targets, switching its attention from the high street to the river coursing through its heart. As the whale reaches Chelsea, building work stops on the hi spec apartments. Everyone, just once in their earthly lifetime, wants to look upon a miracle of nature.

He's tempted himself while he's down here, to drive into central London, join the throng along the banks. Something to tell them all when he gets back. But better just get the job over. Do what he's here for, and head straight back. And after all the whale is not a symbol or a portent – the end time is not upon us, not yet, and when it is much stranger sights will come, beyond imagination – no, the whale is just a frightened beast, confused by the alien sounds churning all around. Why add to the pandemonium? Besides, David hates being in a crowd, belonging to a mob of any kind, even going to the theatre, even taking trains or buses. That's why going to church has always been such an ordeal. But he keeps his seat every Sunday, amongst the congregation, giving thanks for his salvation, so richly undeserved.

Back and forth across the dunes and onto the beach, looking out for a dark jacket with a white circled A on the back. Across the prom and round again, stumbling through sand drifts, sliding down hollows. And still not a soul, barely a footprint. Just the ships going past on their way to Ireland, and a shiver of sandpipers, there and gone.

The first time it was easy. I spotted him right off, leaning against the wind to light up. The beach was where he came to get away from people; he'd spend the whole night on the dunes, wide-awake, immune to the cold.

Sorry to disappoint, but no, he hadn't got anything on him. In fact, so he claimed, I'd slipped his mind completely. 'But you,' he said, looking me over as if he'd never seen me before, 'I think you've got something for me…'

When I finally got into school, just after break, everything seemed different, not real, like a film I was watching, the shapes of the other girls shimmering round the edges, the teachers' mouths out of sync with the sounds they were making. In those days, the teachers let me off, because I'd lost my mother and because I'd never caused them any trouble; and they sentimentally imagined my dad needed me at home

My lips were gritty with sand all afternoon and whenever I took a drink the grains of it swilled in my throat. David hardly touched me. He wasn't like the lads from the boys' school, jamming their hands straight under your bra. But he was in the pores of my skin; I could smell the scent of his body on mine, and I knew that I was already in another place where no one else could reach me.

The meeting takes place in a stuffy suite of offices on an industrial estate, somewhere off the M25. The room's painted greyish blue, with royal blue carpet and chairs, spotless and smelling of acetate. He has never been this close to the elders before, and, though in his job with Parks and Recreation he has regular dealings with MPs and local dignitaries, today he feels as nervous as a man before the judge.

The seven elders, almost identical in their grey suits and wire-rimmed spectacles, listen while he explains the situation once again, concerning the removal of the Christian dead from a neglected cemetery on public graves to make room for a Muslim burial ground. All the implications kept from the public, the minutes of meetings left vague, and the councillors all in thrall to political correctness. But if the Church could step in, and discreetly make an offer…

In the last day I shall rise out of the earth. And I shall be clothed again with my skin, and in my flesh shall I see God.

He is a facts and figures man – facts, figures and faith. *I will lay sinews upon you and will cause flesh to grow over you, and will cover you with skin.* That's what the Bible says; as for theological details, they go way above his head. As the elders debate the complexities, his thoughts are heading back along the motorway already, and inevitably towards Lola.

That defiant smile in Hannah's bedroom. *So? I took five pounds. Big deal. I was going to put it back.*

Stealing from a child's piggy bank – pretty low, don't you think?

She won't miss it. What does she need money for? You buy her everything she asks for. Lola glanced round the pink and white room, with its play tent and dolls' house and piles of soft toys.

'You've broken our trust in you, Lola. Can't you see what you've done?'

Smirking, she pretended to ignore him, hair falling over her face while she carried on with her texting. Even on this chilly January day, Lola dressed like they all did, in low cut jeans accentuated by a wide studded belt and a cropped T-shirt, displaying her navel. Lola was a vegetarian. Living off chocolate and packets of crisps and – he knew, even if she wouldn't admit it – shared bottles of Lambrini, cigarettes and weed –

still she managed to look like a young pop star.

'I'm speaking to you Lola.'

'Yeah, one minute right...'

He snatched the phone, marched to the bathroom and flushed it down the toilet. Lola blinked with shock, but it was little Hannah who screamed, little roly-poly Hannah in her pink nightie, clutching her toy lamb. The phone, of course, did not go down the pan, but it was ruined, and he was not going to buy her another one, she could beg him as much as she liked, go down on her bended knees, made no difference, and Angie wasn't getting her one either, because all this indulgence had just made things worse and if she'd listened to him in the first place...

The arguments went round and round his head, endlessly, as if his wife and stepdaughter were inside, cut round them. Young girls managed fine in the days before mobiles. They were not routinely kidnapped or lured blindly into danger. A mobile phone was not a necessity; it was a plaything, pure and simple. Let her do without for once.

Because Lola wasn't really sorry. Of course, she went through the motions, putting on a glum face instead of the usual self-satisfied grin, turning her voice down to a half-whisper, nibbling broken-heartedly at her plate of chips. Lola provoked him every day of his life. She was utterly shameless. Abandoned to her own pleasure, with no thought for anyone else. She got away with the casual shoplifting, the bunking off school and the lies and the screaming matches because Angie liked to think that this was all a cry for help; Lola was unhappy and confused because she never knew her real dad. But her father had nothing to do with it, not unless you counted the genetic inheritance that made her so invincibly beautiful. She did as she pleased because she thought she was entitled.

Sometimes a kind of night falls and I seem to be asleep. Then I dream about David, holding on to him tight, but still there's no sign. So I keep on looking. What else can I do? I'm not so tired now, or so cold. I watch the wind sweep shimmering patterns over the sand, crossing its surface like the play of light on water. I feel rain on my face or what might be the nip of winter on its way. The sands are constantly changing, damp and spongy underfoot, ribbed as hard as tree roots or blown soft as sugar. The tide goes back and forth, leaving pools and gullies, covering and uncovering broken plastic buckets and jagged bits of wood. And the sea stretches on forever; the Welsh hills and the Wirral seeming to grow increasingly dim as if my eyesight's getting weaker with so much looking. I've seen plenty of footprints, but not their owners, nor even the dogs whose tracks run beside them. One day – how long ago I'm not sure, maybe last week or months past, even years – I realised I'd never once found my own footprint, not once in all the time that I've been waiting for David. The traces are covered up so quickly, when I turn and check they're gone.

He tried to be a good husband and father. In every aspect of his life, great and small, he tried to do the right thing, to atone for his grievous sin. Ever since that terrible morning, he believed that he'd been spared for a purpose – to do some work in the world. It wasn't cowardice that stopped him taking the rest of the pills. He wanted to die when he saw she was gone. But some larger force had stayed his hand. He'd been saved for a reason. And if he was saved then there must be a God. It took several attempts to find the right path, but throughout his sampling of various religions – Buddhism, Paganism, one Christian church and then the next – he kept his promise to be a good man.

When he was plain Church of England, the vicar urged him to go into schools, speaking to teenagers about the perils of drug taking. What could have been more persuasive than first hand experience? He tried but he couldn't. He couldn't face standing up in school assembly. More than that, he couldn't face reliving the horror when Sarah started fitting. He never thought she really meant to kill herself, never thought there were enough pills to do the job, so what was thinking, that it'd be a laugh, that it'd be cool to see what they did to her? He was so off his head, he probably didn't know himself. In those days he was always off his head, moving between different foster homes and then the hostels and the squat in Waterloo. Never had his own place. That was why he liked spending time on the dunes.

Strands of pale hair clogged with sick. Shell fragments crushed against her cheek – her lips a bluish colour – don't think about it. Dismiss her from your mind.

She was a clever girl, into all kinds of crap, books he never heard of, and weird kinds of voodoo – did she make it all up, or read it somewhere? – roping him into all her daft rituals, using candles and incense and photographs of her dead mother. She spooked him sometimes but she turned him on too. She was so incredibly beautiful that for once he actually felt the things that he said – at the time that he said them, he felt them. When they couldn't meet – her dad driving her to and from school, locking the doors of the house – they cast spells by post, exchanging snippets of hair, shells, flower petals – kids' stuff, they were both kids really. And Sarah was reading stories by some German writer who shot himself. It was all in the letters they wrote every day, smuggled back and forth.

Nothing can separate us. Not even death.

He had nightmares for years afterwards, still sometimes dreamt she was swimming – some nowhere place, not the sands, somewhere else, a hotel swimming pool in Spain or Florida – swimming and calling him to take the plunge. *Come on, David, what you waiting for?* But in the dream he couldn't undress, couldn't even unfasten his laces – *Come on, it's really warm* – and when, in some versions, he jumped in fully clothed, he was dragged down beneath the waves, choking on salt water. These terrors were less frequent since he joined the Church and married Angie, and now, if he ever thought about Sarah, it was with the certainty of divine mercy.

He never told Angie what happened to Sarah. All Angie knew was that he'd spent what the Church called a troubled youth, but had put that all behind him long ago. Of course it was pretty obvious that he was what a doctor might label *prone to depression*. For no apparent reason, he'd suddenly go quiet. He'd stop paying attention to the world around him – as if, Angie said, a demon's taken hold of him. She'd grab his hands and speak to him: Look at me. Look at Hannah. Think of our baby. And she wouldn't let him go until he looked back at her with love. Their religion didn't believe in crucifixes, or other outward symbols, so she gave him a ring to wear for those times when she couldn't be with him – a tiger eye. At the first sign, she said, promise me you'll look the tiger in the eye. Think of us. Think of Hannah. And of Our Lord, who walks with you always, even in the shadows.

He tried to keep that promise. But sometimes he was overwhelmed by an unrelenting melancholy, inexorable as a rising tide. What was the cause? Mid-life crisis? Religious doubts? Work (and if the council found out what he told the elders, the risk of losing his job)? Or perhaps the battles with Lola, or the battles about Lola? None of these. No. The demon took hold of him, even now, as his car rolled smoothly down the motorway, in the impulse to let his hands fall from the wheel, close his eyes and yield to death.

Most people don't know what love is. They think it's something that you write on Christmas cards. You can't understand love or explain where it comes from – not real love anyway – like a dream, like magic, like believing there's a God. Most people go to their graves without ever knowing love. Most people have never really been alive. And if you're never lived you're scared to die.

My dad talked about love all the time when I lost the baby. How much my mother loved me and how much he loved her and what she would have wanted. I remember coming to, feeling some one holding my hand and it was my dad, and I didn't have the strength to pull away.

'Sarah,' he kept saying, 'Sarah, you're fine, it's for the best.'

I was in hospital. The one where my mum died. The exact same place.

'Don't be scared. I'm not angry.'

Scared? When was I ever scared? My dad liked to think I was his poor little lamb. And now I was made pure, and the past wiped clean. He brought me some apples and a bunch of flowers and my library books. When the time came to leave he kissed me goodnight, whispering, 'I love you' with tears in his eyes. But I never shed a tear for anyone.

My mother must have lain there too, listening to the rustle of nurses and the squeak of trolley wheels, sleeping and not sleeping in the long twilight between the bedtime Horlicks and the morning cup of tea. I didn't cry for her or for the baby – not a baby, didn't even know I was pregnant, more a seed, a fruit, a kind of jellyfish, a clot washed down the drain – I didn't care. All I thought about was getting out; and if I'd had the strength I would have left and gone to David.

The next morning, some one had taken a bite from the green apple in the fruit bowl. When I opened the book I was reading, *The Marquise of O* by Heinrich von Kleist, there was a letter from David, a letter that said *I will never let you down.* And then I knew I'd sooner die than ever lose him. And no matter what happened, he would always find me.

That was why I didn't argue when my dad came up with this idea about moving to Canada – because I knew that it wasn't going to happen. Everything was fixed. He had a job organised and we could stay with Auntie Margaret. I'd have a wonderful time, and I could still apply to Oxford, or stay over there, even get a scholarship to Harvard, just the place for a bright girl like me...

Soon forget about David. That's what he thought. And I played along, shed a few tears, let him think he was gradually winning me over.

David kept saying, 'You're sure you can go through with it? You won't chicken out?' No. Never. We were going to that place where no one else could find us.

And David? He'd never let me down. He'd never abandon me, leave me to die by myself.

The armies of human kindness are ready, cranes and hoists and pontoons poised to lift the whale and transport him back to sea. Must be quite a sight, but it'll be on telly later, and now, the task performed, he's halfway home. He stabs at the radio buttons, leaving Hilton Park services, fingers still greasy from his KFC. He hates those afternoon plays with their arch BBC voices – and then some weird gargling kind of eastern singing, a hiss of static and tangled foreign tongues – and the play again, that actress with the irritatingly priggish voice – he turns the shape of the name round in his head, but can't quite get it – Iris? Irene? – gives up and jams in a CD at random, heart rising as the beat kicks in. *Ever fallen in love with some one, ever fallen in love, in love with some one, ever fallen in love…*

Life's not so bad. He did the right thing concerning the graveyard. Always does. Tries to do the right thing. *In my flesh shall I see God.* No luck ringing Angie – no answer from the landline and all he gets from the mobile is a distant clatter, probably some shopping centre. He wants to hear her voice so badly, just to tell her everything's okay – everything under control – and not to worry. *In my flesh.*

CAN'T HEAR YOU LOVE, he shouts. IF YOU CAN HEAR ME I'LL BE WITH YOU SOON. GOD BLESS.

Ever fallen in love with some one, ever fallen in love, in love with some one, ever fallen in love… He follows the signs to The North, going along at quite a lick as the dusk starts to thicken. Ever fallen in love with some one, ever fallen in love, in love with some one… Another car pulls in front without signalling, a Mitsubushi Warrior with a sticker in the rear window: BABE ON BOARD! A great blubbery woman sitting up at the wheel – he obliterates his uncharitable thoughts on that subject, but can't stop himself checking her out as he swiftly overtakes, and then she picks up speed again.

David broke his word. There's no other explanation. Any time, any place, David could find me. He sneaked into the hospital. He tracked me down in school; he got those letters to me. Only this time he didn't want to stay with me. He changed his mind.

I gave my life to David. I lost my life for nothing, just to sit here amongst the hunks of rotting timber and the thistles and the jagged pieces of concrete with nails sticking out. Just to sit here waiting like a fool.

Slowly, very slowly, the skies are fading round me, and the shores of New Brighton growing dimmer in the distance. I'm spending longer in that sleepy nighttime state, and whenever I wake up the tide's inching closer. Every time I dream about David, I cling on to him more tightly. Yet it seems to me that in those few seconds his body stiffens and his face turns away. Soon, very soon, I won't see him any more, and I myself will be forgotten, as if I never lived.

I can't let that happen. I can't let myself die. I'll be a voice in the wind, a sound in the rain, a shadow beneath a reflection. I'll stay at his side, biding my time, till he's ready. And then I'll bring him back. I lie still, listening to the surf breaking on the shore, waiting for the turning tide to carry me towards wherever he might be.

Not a soul about. No one home. He knows, before he's even turned the key in the lock, that the house is hollow and empty, the light in the hallway sallow with absence, the telly rattling into a void, the warmth from the central heating dry and stale. He walks though the upstairs, switching on lights, opening cupboards, trying to capture some lingering essence. He picks up an odd sock, flicks through Hannah's reading book – *Cockatoos*, now you see them, now you don't - sniffs the mineral water by Lola's bed, which is actually vodka. Without even thinking, he takes a swig. Nothing. He feels nothing. Tastes of medicine. Another swig, and then he pours it down the plughole.

Tired, bog tired. He turns on the bath taps, the pipes singing, almost drowning the sound of the phone from downstairs.

Angie. At last.

'Where are you?' His own voice sounds feeble and whiny.

'We're on our way – been shopping and we've been to

see *Narnia* – haven't we, Hannah? We're just leaving the Trafford Centre...'

'Where's Lola?'

'She came too,' she says brightly. (So Angie gave in. Bought her a new phone at the Trafford Centre. But he's so tired he doesn't care.) 'We all went to *Narnia*. Want to have a quick word with Hannah?'

The little girl babbles on about the film – ' a what?' he says - 'a LINE, Daddy, a LINE – a line and he was called Aslan and there was a beaver and he was called...'

The TV screen's an intense, funereal black, the Thames by night, the barge on which they carried the whale drifting like an empty slipper, lights dimmed as a sign of respect.

'How you doing, hon?' his wife says softly. 'How was it – listen, traffic's moving off... You did the right thing hon. You're a good man.'

How good to hear her voice at last, to know that he's safely home, shielded from all the dark forces outside. Soon, very soon, the house will be occupied, and the heavy weight that seems to be dragging him down will have gone from his heart. The bathtub's so full he has to let some water out. Black pots from Lush are lined along the shelves, *Dream Cream, Smitten, Lemony Flutter*, Angie's indulgence for giving up sweets – sticky soap bars, bags of sherbetty bombs – *Waving Not Drowning*. In a blue glass bowl, a pile of shells and feathers picked up at Formby, was it, or Southport? Never Crosby. Angie wants to see that art thing, the metal men dispersed across the beach. The pictures give him the creeps, mummified corpses, staring blindly out to sea, something blasphemous about making casts of living bodies, but that's not the real reason why he can't go there.

Outside, the wind is stirring, scattering rain against the windows. Now and then the sounds of passing traffic break like surf. He takes off his watch. Places his tiger's eye ring on the windowsill next to the spider plant. Soon he'll be restored, ready to greet his family, forgiving and forgetting. Even Lola.

He is blessed. God saved him. Brought him back to life when all seemed lost.

The whale died. Went into convulsions and died on the barge. Now everyone says it was for the best. All that effort, all those experts. Killing with Kindness. *We realised we'd have to put her down just before she started to die.* He can't say why those words, even now, bring tears to his eyes, why they've lodged in his mind.

The deep waters welcome him in. He lies there, contemplating the blue and white tiling he put in himself, and it all seems somehow frayed and remote, the outlines of objects ebbing and flowing. *Just before she started to die.* So she was a female. He always thinks of whales as masculine.

He closes his eyes and sinks underwater. He could stay there forever, in the ambient warmth, weightless and remote. 'David?' There's some one in the room. They must be home already. 'David?' A gentle, quizzical voice, a young girl's voice. He knows that voice. The voice of a demon. He lies still and listens till he can't hold his breath much longer. He doesn't want to come to the surface till the demon has left him. But he never does get up. His heart is weighted like a stone, filled with the sweet melancholy he has come to love almost as much as God. *Think of us, think of Hannah.* But he can't. And he will never hear the banging on the bathroom door or the child's desperate wail on the landing.

THIS IS HOW DANGER APPROACHES ME

Georgina Parfitt

From this window, the trees are Jurassic. That one is flat on the top making a home for vultures. That one has four green crowns, each swaying carefully as if keeping, in its thickness, a family of unhatched eggs.

I have to imagine the breeze that's making the trees move like that, because I certainly can't feel it from here. The window has been closed for days and the heat has settled in the room. There are flowers on the windowsill but they've done their growing. All they have is colour.

*

I have been on bed rest. I had the kind of breakdown that the family doctor described as 'par-for-the-course'. I told Everly that I needed to have some soup and sleep it off for an afternoon, but this was last week. Something is happening. I'm not sure what.

Everly is a good daughter. Solid and quiet, she comes in and out of the room and tells me something she read in the paper.

The longer she is out in the world, the more her own mannerisms develop; now she has her own way of holding things, all of her fingers nervously engaged in the task. She carried the flowers in a few days ago and arranged the stems after putting them on the windowsill.

She is out at the post office now and so I watch the trees. And because I can only see the tops, I can imagine that there is a savannah below, stretching out, grassless, uninhabited wasteland.

These trees are a kind of conversation. In the same way that Everly will nod and respond, nod and respond, the trees nod and respond.

They appear when I look towards the window, expecting my trouble. I find myself feeling sad when they start to darken in the evenings and the wind moves them further and back, as if they've become distracted and have stopped listening to me.

*

There is nothing like natural light. Inside, the lamp glows like neon. Outside, the sky is turning grey and yet there's more light out there than in here, somehow. Even the seagulls that cross this way and that have light in them, hovering each one like a moon before passing on.

*

Everly must have been caught by a talker at the post office. You can run into anybody there, an old teacher, the family doctor, just somebody wanting to talk.

And Everly is fascinated by men, having been only small when her spitting image her own father 'disappeared', as they say. Any time I've seen her with them, she fawns and watches. When I was her age, I was the same. Many entries of my diary were dedicated to men I knew. Sometimes I would just list them, alongside their major attributes. Black hair. Athletics club. And so on. But it was a long time before I really knew a man.

The one I chose to know first was my husband, the man that gave Everly her name; it was the most consideration he ever gave anything, of what I witnessed.

Oh my daughter, I sometimes say in my head when I am sympathising with her.

She will always be so much younger than I am – her bare legs stomping into the room, bringing in a tray of food she's cooked. Every part of the meal, from the small, peeled potatoes to the neat slice of pie (the filling escapes as she places it down on the table) has something of the novice about it.

Sometimes she takes so long at the post office that I think she might have got married and started a family in one of the nearby towns.

The flat-topped tree blows.

There is finally a chill that comes into the room. Though from what direction I can hardly tell. The window is shut tight and warm.

Could it possibly be coming from the ceiling? The roof must be very thin. We have no attic.

*

And what would her marriage look like?

Good heavens. I don't even know if her husband will be handsome. Will Everly have a handsome husband? Is she beautiful, my daughter?

I wish I still had my wedding dress. In one day outside in the fields where we had the reception it became yellow as the milkweed, seams yellow, lace yellow, veil yellow.

But Everly's blond hair would make it look quite deliberate.

I like to think she could have a kind husband at least. One who would kindly seat me in his own favourite chair when I came over to visit. We'd have arranged to watch a show together. He would ask me if I still like to have a drink in the evening and will I have one with him.

Now on the other side of the tree, the sun hits. It has just

dog to sleep. She took quick, useless showers and brushed her hair in my bedroom.

*

I'd better try to sleep, I think, to pass the time. So I shift over to the other side of the bed and reach the light switch. I see the glow of the overhead lamp spiral and then, like I've had an aesthetic, the room cuts out.

The window soon appears though, blue, like a kind of back-up electricity at one of those underground nightclubs if you look down along a street in a European city. Through the grate you can just about see an arm, a pale moving arm of a woman and the air along the street being blown around by the air conditioner.

And the groups sitting outside a restaurant further on looking out at the square drinking beer and smoking seem to be in association with the figures in the night club, as with the waiters in the restaurant, the handsome man sitting on the rickshaw and the chef on the back step with his shoes off.

*

There are no restaurants around here. I imagine Everly sitting on an iron chair with her strong legs out, relaxed as if she's drunk. This is a different Everly from the one who's married with a four-poster bed and a kind, plain husband. And different from the Everly who's lying in a stream.

I reach out to turn the light on again but my fingers find the cold flat wall instead.

After that I can't settle in either light or dark. Each one is lacking the other. A time comes when you have to do something. You have to choose what that thing is.

The trees blow in the dark, over goodness knows what kind of place. In my mind are black old nests blowing like a plague along the ground, or a makeshift civilisation of little twig houses along the bare clay bank of a stream. All of this in the dark. The trees blowing.

Animals coming from far off to slow down and lower themselves into the water and slowly bathe their thick skins.

The dinner party is probably at the sprawling stage, and the scholar takes up most of the sofa, no longer embarrassed to be pouring herself tiny glass after tiny glass of the expensive port they've brought out for the occasion.

What would she say if she turned around on the sofa to see me outside looking for my lost daughter? Me in the dark like those old trees. My hair and robe blown back.

She would probably compare me to something she's read.

Under the covers, I gather my robe with both hands, ready for the gust of wind.

I find the corner of the covers and lift them away carefully. It is already cold. I shudder and find myself standing – reeling – suddenly, with my hand on the blue windowsill, pulling myself into the room, avoiding the mirror, slipping my feet into shoes – even I remember how to look civilised – finding the door, and swinging it, toddling into the hallway – the whole house dark – I stop for a moment.

The house rings with what I've just done.

And what have I done?

At my wedding, I thought my feet had turned to stone as I stood at the beginning of the aisle. When I first held Everly in my arms, I tried to count to three before looking at her so I was ready, but I accidentally looked on two.

The light from the porch is shining onto the carpet. As I open the front door and step out, our asphalt driveway is lit from above by the security light. I wait in the glare. The wind blows cold. Then the light turns itself off.

Now it is so dark that I think I almost see the savannah, stretching out, uninhabited, but it is another row of houses. Bricks, windows, tiny trees in a row, porch, wind chime. I stand looking out at it. I step out into the driveway. I am dark as everything else.

I wonder what I'll look like standing, robe blowing, in the dark. I wonder how I'll explain it.

SHADOWS

Robert Anthony

The man walked into the sunshine with his automatic shadow following him. He'd received it from the religion people down at the mall, they were giving away free shadows to the first one thousand to walk into the light, which, as he understood, meant simply walking down the sidewalk in front of the Tastee Squeeze, just before you got to Hardee's, which is where they'd set up their booth, just to walk in the sunshine a little ways, and now he had a shadow that would follow him all the time, whenever there was light to remind him of the true path. 'Without light you will have no shadow,' the man told him, reminding him that no gift comes without conditions. But he accepted this, because he was without anything else in which to believe. He was a man whose condition was that of bare subsistence in the world. 'Many plants and animals just get by, and I don't know that I am better than they are.'

He went home. His wife was waiting there, cooking a dead animal in a pot. She'd added: cumin, garlic, ginger, yogurt, coriander, and a lot of other things. The main ingredients of the dish were the animal's flesh, the animal's bones, onions, the spices mentioned above, and death. Death was the secret ingredient. Without death there would have been no dish, because the animal would have jumped right out of the pot and they would have been left with a messy kitchen and an animal screeching around the apartment, burned and covered in sauce. Once an animal is out of the pot and screeching around the apartment, it's no longer dinner, but something between a nuisance and a danger. There's little chance it will become a pet, once you've tried to eat it. In any case, his wife had added death to the dish, which she kept in a jar by the stove, right next to the salt. Like salt, you could barely taste death, or, really, not taste it at all. It simply added flavour to the dish, although, once, when he was drunk, he'd tasted it right from the jar, and it tasted somewhat minty, quite a bit minty, like fresh herbs. This surprised him, because he'd always assumed it would be musty or bitter, but death was quite refreshing, in the end, and he told his wife to add more death to her dishes, and she'd said she would, although he wasn't sure, in the end, if she did.

'Dead animal tonight?' he said as he walked in and kissed her.

'Of course,' she said. 'With more death, just like you like it.'

'Good,' he said. And it was. He went to his room and took off his shadow. The people at the religion had told him it was fine to do this, but that he should try to lay it out flat, for a wrinkled shadow in an invitation to demons, or no, that was simply what he had thought they'd said – what had they said? He took out the pamphlet they'd given him and tried to read the little print in the dim light. There was nothing on it, and then he remembered that they'd said the writings of the church of sunshine could only be read in sunshine, which seemed to him to a bad idea, because the people they should most want to reach would be those in shadow. But then he wasn't a priest, so what did he know? In any case he pressed the shadow flat until he could barely feel it between his fingers, it was only a sliver of darkness, thinner than silk. Only too late did he begin to realize that it was sinking into his fingers, immediately turning them dark, and from there: his hands, his forearms. A sudden image came into his mind: 'I am water into which ink has been poured.'

He sat for a moment on the bed. He'd ruined the shadow. He'd pressed it too hard and it had simply disappeared. Ah well, it was a nice thing to have while it lasted, an automatic shadow. He'd really enjoyed the way it attached itself to him and mimicked and distorted his motions. What a marvel of engineering it was! He realized he was crying, a little, a few tears flowing down his cheeks. He wiped them away and got up.

'Oh my god,' his wife said. 'What's happened?'

'What's happened?'

'Your face, your – all of you, it's black.'

'Black?'

'Grey.'

'Oh,' he said, 'I see.' And he did. He looked down at his hands. They were charcoal-stained with his dried tears. It was pretty predictable, really, the way these things worked. Sometimes the world was so literal. Now he'd become neither man nor shadow, but something in between, neither the refreshing darkness, nor the loving sun. He was simply the grey of the inside of a sardine can. You glance at it once before you throw it away.

'Would you like some dinner, dear?' his wife asked him after a while.

'Sure,' he said.

But he took no pleasure in it. It was tasteless, not the dish, but the death, like always, but for once he wanted to taste death in everything he did.

Later they made love, and he squirted a little death inside her, so that her belly quivered and she got a funny look on her face, as if some child had appeared for a moment, then disappeared, unborn.

'Are you OK?' he said.
'I came so hard.'

That night, while she slept, he got up and ate all the death in the jar, and for a moment he felt resolved, oblivion-filled. Out the window, over the water: the grey light of dawn rising over the freeway, the hum of a truck out there on the interstate moving through the early morning fog, and below: his hands in the grey light, holding the empty jar, the grey jar with the grey emptiness in his thin grey hands. He stepped forward, off the porch, into the distant night that started right here, looking to fill up the jar.

~~GREAT EXPECTATIONS~~

~~Charles Dickens~~

THE NOVEL FACTORY

Luke Melia

'My father's family name being Pirrip, and my Christian name Philip, my infant tongue could make of both names nothing longer or more explicit than Pip. So, I called myself Pip, and came to be called Pip.'

My humble apologies dear reader, but there is no further text from esteemed author Charles John Huffan Dickens in this edition of his 1861 classic tale *Great Expectations*. I am most aggrieved to inform you that the copy of his noble novel you have purchased was found damaged in the Rapti River by local businessman, Amid Bhatka.

To divulge, Amid Bhakta is a short man who smokes *Kuchary* cigarettes and wears a *Chicago Bulls* baseball cap. He is what the Americans call an entrepreneur and sees money in everything, everywhere. When he discovered three large boxes of books in the Rapti River on Tuesday afternoon, all he could think about were the rupees they might be worth.

Sadly, the damage to the cargo was substantial. Just two of the boxes had remained intact, their wealth of stories somewhat less spoiled than the drowned pages. Of the books that were saved, I can reveal that only the hard covers and opening words survived their encounter with the river water.

Howsoever, Amid Bhakta is a determined man. After failing to bake the works dry in the sun, he settled on a new plan of action. He has enlisted the help of myself, Aditya Singh of Chitwan, Nepal, and my friend, Janak Mitra, also of Chitwan, Nepal, to repair the great literature.

Amid Bhakta has commissioned us to recreate each title from original texts found on the Internet. We are instructed to format the stores into *Microsoft Word* documents so that they can be rebound into the original hard covers by Amid Bhakta's brother-in-law in India. We are promised a share in any profits made by the enterprise.

Therefore, Janak has embarked on the reconstitution of Jane Austen's *Pride and Prejudice* (1813), Herman Melville's *Moby Dick* (1851), and Mary Shelley's *Frankenstein* (1818). While my privilege is Charlotte Bronte's *Jane Eyre* (1847), Herbert George Wells' *The War of the Worlds* (1898) and the recovery of Mr Dickens' fine story of Pip, a narrative I am most familiar with, having read the text with full satisfaction only six months ago.

Unfortunately, our task will consume a considerable number of hours. The recovery of the books is currently being performed by manual word processing. It cannot be achieved through the *Microsoft Word* tools 'Copy' and 'Paste,' as first proposed. Our *Microsoft Word* programme is not so good. I am of suspicion that it has not been paid for and does not function to full capacity.

Amid Bhakta has assured us that he shall be addressing our technical issues. Regrettably, we are aware that he does not wish to spend a single rupee to rectify the faults and is attempting to borrow a full version of the software from his father's cousin's business partner. Negotiations are ongoing.

In conclusion, it is my pleasure to announce that we have made a decision to rebel against the business venture and write original narratives that will top the *New York Times'* bestseller list.

We have converted a small room above Amid Bhakta's electronical goods emporium into what has come to be called our novel factory, a name I created to honour Mr Dickens' most ingenious of brains.

Once again, my sincere apologies for the inconvenience. I would like to make a promise of every endeavour to enthral you. I am most honoured to be writing in English, the language of William Shakespeare and Dan Brown. It is my best subject at college, and actually the reason I was chosen for this task by Amid Bhakta.

I am truly thrilled by the secret undertaking and so too is Janak. He has promptly set upon writing a children's classic about a young boy from Chitwan who discovers the entrance to a supernatural world. The gripping plot includes talking dinosaurs, flying machines, and the triumph of good over evil.

I am pleased to report that I will be penning a more learned book. My own desire is to write about Nepal. I wish to explain everything that I see in my country, the good and the bad. I am certain I am fit to burst with a saga that will give the world the wondrous spirit of my country, and then reveal how this precious spirit has grown so sick and troubled in recent times.

Here I begin…

*

It is with great sorrow that I must report a hindrance. I confess I do not know where to start my yarn of Nepal. I have discovered that knowing the essence of a book is not enough. I am enlightened by a publisher's website that you must create an array of colourful characters which come alive off the page. It is my misfortune to suspect such a feat is beyond my abilities.

I am also experiencing a problem with concentration. As I write, *Microsoft Word* informs me of a number of critical errors in this document. I have relayed the state of affairs to Amid Bhakta on numerous occasions but he does not care in the slightest. It would seem he is no closer to procuring legitimate software.

So much for him. Amid Bhakta and his counterfeit *Microsoft* product are indeed the least of my misery. I am now in love with my new teacher, Jessica Hanson. She is from Manchester in England and has recently arrived on the *Local World Heroes* volunteer scheme.

Jessica smells of fragrant sun moisturiser. She has the looks of Hollywood actress and English rose, Kate Winslet, sporting blonde curly hair, blue eyes, and a pale but healthy complexion with no zits or blemishes to note. Her smile is her finest feature. It sparkles across her face and radiates splendour as when she was introduced to our class and received a thunderous round of applause.

In less than a week, Jessica has become the apple of every eye in Chitwan. Janak boasts that her stare regularly rests upon him in class. He has proclaimed that he shall dedicate his children's classic to her honour. Several other suitors, including a number of wedded villagers, have also claimed her as a true love.

Woefully, I am unable to compete for her hand. I have made a disastrous first impression on the fair Jessica. Firstly, I was humiliated when she posed a question to me in English grammar studies.

'So Aditya, can you tell me where the verb is in this sentence?' she asked.

The sentence on the blackboard was: 'In early October, Lale will plant more rice.' I knew at once that a verb expresses actions, or events, and in this case, 'will plant,' constituted the verb in the sentence and correct answer to Jessica's question.

Howsoever, my small brain and loud mouth conspired against me and the word 'October' fell from my lips, causing raucous amusement among my classmates. I flushed warm with embarrassment and was actually unable to speak to rectify my error.

Jessica hushed the class. Her face was full of kindness as she explained the principle of a verb once more, and kept her wonderful gaze on me for the time. Little was I to know, the exhilaration of such attention would be short-lived.

Events occurred to further ruin of my standing with this enchanting girl.

To explain, I must divulge that my father is an accountant for a tourist jungle lodge within the boundaries of the national park of Chitwan. In recent months, I have been performing some work duties on certain occasions after college. This day, I was to visit the lodge to aid the fumigation of rooms.

I had no sooner commenced my assigned sector of guest huts when I happened upon Jessica. I was stunned to witness her sitting in front of a lodge room with a note journal. She was crying.

I did not have time to speak before she discovered me. We looked upon each other in startled-shock.

'Aditya!' she cried.

'Excuse me,' I answered and pray now I had not been so cowardly as to turn and stride away.

I was troubled beyond measure by the encounter. The anger at the faintness of my heart intoxicated my brain. I have concluded that it led to temporary madness for I went on to commit a most despicable act of treachery.

I awaited to hear that Jessica had been called to dinner before returning to her lodge room. The door was locked but I entered with ease. The latches are a simple device to unpick once shown the method.

I immediately located the aim of my wicked action. Jessica's note journal was on her bed and I am ashamed to disclose that I read every page.

I was consumed with the desire to uncover the reason for her sadness and was duly informed by the delicate handwriting. Jessica is homesick. She longs for a place called Salford and her mother and brother, and makes several threats to fly home within the next forty-eight hours.

You see, it is a catastrophe. I know what is troubling Jessica. It is the sick spirit of Nepal. The spirit I wish to write about. This should certainly not be and I am burdened with the enormity of the knowledge.

I conclude that I must take responsibility for my country and make Jessica wish to stay. Yet one whole day has since gone by and I remain at a loss as to how I shall fulfil my task.

I have therefore decided to seek the advice of the wisest person in Chitwan, Doctor Harka…

*

Forgive me, I am typing at speed. Amid Bhakta has struck a deal with a printer in Kathmandu which has made time of the greatest essence. I have approximately one half hour to complete my composition before he returns to inspect full copies of the fine works of literature.

Tragically, this signals the end of our novel factory. The agreement includes the provision of an authorised edition of *Microsoft Word* with full 'Copy' and 'Paste' functions enabled. I have an online text of *Great Expectations* ready for insertion into this document. Howsoever, I intend to be conniving and smuggle my own tale into the finished manuscript, undetected.

I sought out the advice of Doctor Harka, an eminent jungle man from one of the oldest families in Chitwan. Doctor Harka is held in the highest esteem. He is a trained western physician and bears a striking resemblance to Bollywood superstar Amitabh Bachchan.

He answered my description of events with a smile.

'Show her a tiger,' he said.

'A tiger?' I was utterly bewildered.

'She wishes for something incredible to happen. Make a tiger happen. The experience will cure her homesickness.'

'But I do not have time,' I despaired. 'There is only one day before she intends to fly home.'

Doctor Harka continued his smile. He waved his hand for me to follow him. I followed. He led me to a small cupboard and pointed inside.

I was perplexed to be confronted by a brightly coloured tiger costume hanging on the handle of a broomstick.

'Point at a deer and call it a horse,' he said.

In spite of the deepest reservations at the proposed course of deceit, I did not have time or intelligence to create a superior scheme. Therefore, I transpired events so Jessica was invited on an evening jungle walk. In shame, I lay in wait for her along the track, dressed in the tiger suit.

If this circumstance did not make me feel sufficiently foolish, to instigate the plan I had been forced to confide the scheme to Janak. Thankfully, his amusement was tempered by the seriousness of the situation.

He agreed that it was imperative to make Jessica stay in Nepal and did not mock me once I was fully dressed up in the cumbersome outfit.

'The colours are quite authentic,' he commented.

'It smells foul,' I grumbled as I placed the headpiece over my shoulders. It was heavy and highly compromised my ability to see.

'Do not complain,' Janak rebuked. 'I will whistle to announce our arrival at the viewing platform.'

I nodded my understanding and adjusted the eye sockets. I took up position to wait at the base of a cotton tree, highly aggrieved by the ordeal I was suffering.

An eternity of time elapsed before the signal arrived. The sound surprised me for I had embarked on a wondrous daydream wherein I was married to Jessica and we lived together amongst the magical surroundings of Salford. I believe this distraction alongside my poor vision in the tiger headpiece, were the reasons I did not notice the rhinoceros.

It was a thoroughly terrifying turn of events. The mighty beast was actually less than fifteen feet away and observed at me with grave suspicion. I wish I could say that I acted the brave man or a cool customer. I did not.

Jessica and the plan vanished from my mind. I ran as fast as I could in the heavy attire towards the viewing platform. In my haste, the tiger head was flung behind me and I could not help urinating inside my own underwear. I failed to pause for breath until I was met with a fate worse than trampling.

At the viewing platform, there was a large crowd of onlookers to greet me with raucous amusement. I spied Janak standing with Jessica, a most triumphant grin across his face.

The horror became apparent. The villain had double-crossed me and spoken out about my plan.

I was swiftly surrounded by laughing faces and heartless comments at my comical appearance. My attempts to fight through them were futile. I resigned myself to the jeers and wished for death.

The lodge did not quickly tire of its merriment. I was trailed to my father's cabin and could hear howls of laughter while I scrubbed urine from the costume. I am not ashamed to tell that I wept a river of tears and wished to inflict harm on Janak in most hideous acts of violence.

I changed my clothes and attempted to wipe the stinging from my eyes. I was considering the requirement to retrieve the tiger headpiece when there was a knock at the door.

I froze, fearful of further torment.

'Aditya?' I could not believe my ears. It was Jessica. 'Aditya, look at me,' she said.

My heart was full of a thousand aches and I hid myself in the towel. I felt her hand arrive at my shoulder and could not help but tremble.

She turned me to her and kissed me on the mouth. Her lips were soft, like cotton, and she smelt of the jungle in early morning dew. I shivered yet was burning hot inside.

'Janak told me you did this for me,' she spoke quietly. 'Thank you. You have shown me how to be brave.'

She held me in the most perfect embrace. I am unable to recall for how long it lasted. I can only say that I wished for it to last forever.

When I opened my eyes, Jessica had gone. I did not look upon her face even a single second. I am now fearful that my imagination has cruelly tricked me and our encounter did not happen. I am praying for the courage to visit Jessica this evening. Indeed, I must warn her of the sick spirit of Nepal. It is of the utmost importance that I now protect her.

Howsoever, my story must end here. There are footsteps upon the stairs. It announces the arrival of Amid Bhakta. My time is up. I shall return you to Mr Dickens' classic tale of Pip and Miss Havisham.

My humble apologies once more for this interruption to your reading pleasure. I click now at the 'Paste' option...

THE GIRL

Victoria Hattersley

She walked through the station entrance at the same time every day. Sometimes he thought that was what he most liked about her. If they'd asked him, 'What is it about this girl you find so appealing?' he might even have answered, 'Well, the main thing is she's quite impressively punctual.'

But of course it wasn't just that. Sometimes as she tried to go through the ticket barriers they wouldn't work. Ticket barriers are like that. She'd become slightly flustered and study her ticket with a puzzled expression. This would almost invariably bring the men who worked at the barriers hurrying over to her. Sometimes it was the older one with the limp. Sometimes it was the younger one who thought he was better than he was. Obvious from the way he chewed gum. They liked to help her. He could see. They liked to watch the way her laugh transformed her face. She would push strands of hair away from her eyes with her hand. Flirting slightly, maybe. But not too much.

She wasn't beautiful, exactly. Nobody could call her that. But she tied her hair back in such a way that it took on a life of its own when she walked quickly. And when she smiled, which she did quite often, it spread across her whole face. Her teeth were white and very even. Clean.

He only noticed this because he himself didn't like to smile too often. He'd tried it in front of the mirror once as an experiment and he'd found himself faintly disturbed. He looked alarming, predatory even though he wasn't.

Once, something had fallen from her handbag as she was buying an overpriced coffee from the stand. For a moment he had almost been the one who picked it up for her. He thought about hurrying forward and handing the object to her, whatever it was – a receipt, a lipstick, a note even. She would smile at him and say, 'Thanks'. And then, 'Don't you get a train every day as well?' But he spent just a second too long picturing her face as she looked at him. Grateful. Somebody else got there first and he could only look on in defeat.

That morning she'd had no trouble getting through the ticket barriers. He watched her miraculously high heels, heard them click-clicking as she walked towards her train. There were other sounds of course. It was a station. There were trains pulling in, announcements over the tannoy, the chatter of pigeons and a couple in the corner squabbling over something that couldn't have mattered. Or didn't matter to him. This amounted to the same thing. In any case, all he really heard was her heels. Over everything else, that's what transmitted its way through to his brain. Brittle sound waves shooting over like a code for him to unravel. He believed in codes. That if you only had the key to something you owned it.

But he didn't have the key to her. And he felt somehow that he ought to.

Maybe after today he would. When she got off the train that evening, left the station and just before she turned right as she did every day. That's when he was going to do it.

Last night, the hooker had taken a long time to die. Normally it took a couple of swift jabs to the stomach or chest area and down they went. To him, this one was being unfair. She wasn't playing the game. She was cursing at him. Outraged. And gesticulating wildly with her arms. It was almost startling.

Chris shoved him urgently in the arm. 'What are you doing? Just get in the car. The Russians are getting away with the explosives.'

He ignored Chris. He couldn't leave her alive now. Even if he got the explosives in time there'd be unfinished business. He'd have to go back and find her again. Or one that looked like her. Most of them looked the same. They'd been designed that way.

Of course, her obscene objections did eventually end. Then he got back into the car he'd taken from the deliveryman a few blocks back down the road. He set off to get the explosives, although Chris was right. It was probably too late by now. Already he could see, on the map in the corner of the screen, the green marker that indicated the Russians' car was reaching its destination. Fuck it anyway. He threw down the controller.

'I think I'm going to talk to a girl,' he said.

Chris stared at the control. 'Have you given up on this one? Want me to take over?'

'Yes, you try. I think I've got hand cramp.'

Chris picked it up. 'Why tell me that anyway? You must talk to girls all the time at work. I do. Every day.'

'Yes, but… Never mind. Forget I said anything.' He frowned, scratching at the flaking patches of skin around his nose. Some of it fell like scales.

Chris wouldn't understand it anyway, he realised now. He shouldn't have said anything, except that for some reason he'd wanted to share it with someone. Anyone. And really, there wasn't anyone else.

His decision had come as something of a surprise to himself. After all these weeks, months – years, even – it was like a light going on in a dark room. Like looking up into the night sky and seeing Orion's belt through a single break in the clouds.

There was a problem, he admitted to himself when the evening came, as he stood studying the poster outside the newsagents.

It was a movie poster – George Clooney and somebody else – and it was reassuringly the same every day. Except today. One corner of it had come slightly loose and it was curling over. There was an old poster left fading underneath and it was trying to reassert itself. It bothered him. As he kept an eye on the platform for her his fingers worked surreptitiously, trying to fix it back into position.

And the problem was this: he didn't know the protocol for talking to someone. People talked to *him* all the time. Asking him to fix a problem with their computer at work, for example. Chris asking him if he wanted to go for a drink. But now that he came to think of it, in all his years he'd never really talked *to* someone. All by himself. There was a difference that he'd failed to notice, and so he'd never learned.

She'd looked at him once, he remembered. He'd been standing in just this spot and she'd walked past him on her way to the exit. Just before she reached him, she'd paused, and looked back towards the emptying platform. As if searching for someone or trying to remember something. Then whatever had held her thoughts, it went. She pivoted on her heels and her large eyes fastened on him. Up close, he could see they were a greenish-blue. Possibly. Or was it just the light? The look lasted easily for a second but could have been longer. Enough time to register his features as those of a real person. She'd given a partial smile.

As she walked away that day he scratched at his face, vaguely hating it, and looked down. For a moment he almost imagined he saw a pile of his skin lying on the floor. Fallen ashes. But then his mind adjusted and he saw it was a stained napkin from the coffee stand.

And now he stood by George Clooney and waited as her train finally came in. He'd thought about what he might say most of last night and all that day. And of what she might say in return. If he said the right thing she'd see through his skins. Each layer of him that wasn't him. She'd understand. She frightened him.

The passengers got off; his eyes scanned through them to find her.

More and more of them hurried past him, wanting their evenings to begin. He shifted his feet, running his fingers up and down George Clooney's face.

Then, there she was. Click clack. She walked past him. He gave what he felt was a decent few seconds (he didn't want her to feel his breath on her neck) and followed after her, upping his pace as she reached the main doors and made her usual right turn. In his sudden, unaccustomed haste he stumbled a little on the frayed hem of his jeans.

'Excuse me.' He thought he had got the tone right. Not urgent. Enquiring. Casual almost. It was a successful conversational opener. Nobody could have suggested otherwise.

Except that she carried on walking. Fatally, he realised, he had not made it clear enough that he was trying to get her attention, and hers alone. Perhaps he had not been in the correct radius or sphere to pull her in. Conversational orbit, was that it? As he found himself considering whether this was the right term he realised that she was getting away onto the road. She would soon be making her second right turn of the evening. He had to quicken his pace.

'Excuse me!'

She jumped, gasped, and her head swivelled round. At the same time her hand went to the strap of her bag over her shoulder. He had overdone it and got too close. And he had lost control of the volume of his voice. It was unfortunate but he had to admit to himself what he had done: ran up to her and shouted in her ear.

'Hi?'

She eyed him with what may have been something like caution, but was not exactly unfriendly. Could he see curiosity? Intrigue? He had never stood close to her for this length of time. Some of her eyelashes were clogged together with black. He wanted to separate them.

'I just wondered whether... I mean we both come here every day...'

'Do we?'

'Yes. I get the train to work. Every day for the past three years.'

'Oh. OK. Yes, so do I.' She smiled, finally. Maybe a little too brightly. For a second her strong white upper incisors bit down on her bottom lip. The place where they'd locked down filled with colour. She glanced around her quickly. Why? He could feel himself becoming agitated. His face itched.

'It's getting dark now and... do you like the stars?'

'Sorry?'

'No. I meant, do you want a coffee one day? When you get off your train?' He forced the words out in quick fire.

'Oh… Listen, it's really nice of you. It is. But I'm not sure my boyfriend would like it, and in any case, I don't have a lot of time in the evenings.'

'OK. I'm sorry. Stupid to ask really. I just – thought I'd see. I'd better let you go.'

He turned to walk away and felt a hand on his arm. He looked back at her. Was that pity he saw in her eyes? Or regret?

'Don't be sorry. It was nice of you to ask. I'm not being rude it's – well that's just the way things are. Thank you anyway. Maybe see you another time.'

She turned and walked away, briskly. He saw her reach into her pocket, take out her phone and begin tapping the screen. Whoever she'd called answered quickly. He heard a burst of laughter. To his ears it was suddenly harsh. Abrasive.

He rubbed the place where her hand had touched his arm. Then he gripped it hard. It was glowing. He found that breathing was difficult and took a few moments to rectify this. Then he went after her. He just wanted to know where she went next.

Later on, when he got home. When he thought about it. He felt that he had committed a crime.

He didn't want to go to work for a week or so after that evening. When he came back and waited in the usual place, she didn't appear. But there was no one he could ask to find out where she had gone. George Clooney was gone too. He'd been replaced by a poster of a blonde woman with a glossy smile. Somehow he didn't want to stand next to her.

The next day, she still wasn't there. And the day after that. And the next. The lack of her made him uneasy. Could any of the people around him see that something had changed? He became aware that he was straining to hear the sound of her absent heels. He tried to concentrate on other sounds. But they were ugly. Muddy. All thrown in together to form a single, gigantic howl. He knew the world was a threatening place.

On the seventh morning, as his train pulled away, he looked back at the receding track. For a moment – it could have been a tic of the brain – he saw what looked like a body. Violently hurt. Man or a woman, he couldn't be sure. Or maybe, he thought, it was simply a mound of skin shed by someone – or something – that no longer needed it. Slippery. Already putrefying.

A dying star sheds its skin. He remembered this, as he lay on the narrow ledge outside his flat and stared at the neat patterns in the sky. He was glad, mostly, that nobody ever came here. He believed in distances, like he believed in codes. Seen from far away, things have order.

Or course, it's really just the star's atmosphere it's shedding. Beautiful, glowing lobes of gas that drift around for a while before it's all gone. Forever. He recalled the unaccustomed thrill he'd felt, all those years ago, when he learned all this. Suddenly his physics teacher wasn't just a nervous man who was too young for the beard he wore. Through him there came a voice from another place. Where there was nothing but distances.

Once or twice he'd tried to tell Chris about this, but stars weren't his thing. And really, there was no-one else to tell. He thought maybe he would have liked to tell her about it.

It hadn't been a crime.

POWER SURGE

Graeme Finnie

It was late afternoon by the time Johnny Miller finished at the Institute. He backed into the doorway of 1724 Main Street, pulled a crumpled pack of Camels from his pocket and lit his last one. He cupped the smoke close in his hand and caught the flare of the match before a gust of wind snuffed it out.

'Phonies,' he exhaled.

He glanced over his shoulder. The whole thing was shaky. He should've seen through it. The 'Professor' guy, Davidson, seemed genuine enough, except he'd been watching and listening like Mr Sneaky skulking in the corner; Hoffman, the instructor, was stiff and cold like a mortician's model; McMurphy, the one supposed to be learning it all, with his 'Let me out... I can't go on,' the son of a bitch was an actor. He took a deep draw on the smoke.

Something caught at the back of his throat, like a burr. He coughed, then tossed the half-smoked butt away. He was spluttering like a kid trying them for the first time. The ones he'd had in there, after the 'Professor' had come in to try and calm the situation, tasted rubbery, like they'd been rolled from inner tubes. He massaged his arm where he'd been wired up: it pulsed as if he was still connected.

Traffic crawled past like it was being dragged along on chains. When a gap opened up he cut across to the drug store opposite to buy a fresh pack of smokes. Further up the block there was a crowd huddled under the canopy outside Loews Theatre for *The Manchurian Candidate*. He'd seen it with some ex Navy guys from work that had been in Korea. They said it didn't wash: you couldn't brainwash a bunch of American GIs who were brainless to begin with and anyway, a more serious point, nobody could make you do things against your will.

Johnny Miller reckoned he had a different slant on it now. You could fix it so people would do those things.

*

He'd found the notice tucked away in the bottom corner on an inside page of the *Bridgeport Telegram* about two weeks earlier.

PUBLIC ANNOUNCEMENT
WE WILL PAY YOU $4.00
FOR ONE HOUR OF YOUR TIME

Persons Needed for a Study of Memory

The Institute of Applied Memory Research (conducting research on behalf of industry) is looking for volunteers for a scientific study of memory and learning.
Each volunteer will be paid $4.00 (plus 50c carfare) for approximately 1 hour's time.
There are no further obligations and no special training, experience or qualifications are required.
You may choose the time you wish to attend.
If you would like to participate please fill out and return the attached coupon.

He sat at the dresser in his bedroom in the rooming house with the coupon in front of him. The silvering on the mirror was fading, its edges eroding like a coastline and dark flecks like distant islands spotted the glass. It seemed like $4.00 for not doing much, and he figured his memory was pretty good. He filled it in. Any time away from Global Brakes was time well spent.

The call came through to his desk in the drawing office a couple of days after he mailed it. Drawings for a new line of components, some military job, were unrolled over the worktop and weighted down with a couple of brake shoes, rejects from the foundry. He was expecting a call from the print room about a set of drawings he had requested. He had already sent them back twice because of mistakes.

'Yeah… Got those drawings for me yet?'

'Pardon?' A voice he didn't recognise.

'Hello… Who is this?'

'I'm calling for Mr Miller… Have I got the wrong number?'

'No… You got the right number… I was expectin' another call. Say is this about the,' dropping his voice, 'memory test?'

Beyond the rain-streaked windows of the drawing office a pair of bulldozers were crawling across the muddy lot at the back of the plant, levelling it for a new public housing project. As they manoeuvred around the lagoons that scarred its surface, waves of earth curled on the lips of their steel blades. The work, which was months behind schedule, had started in the summer when the office was like a hothouse and they had to keep the windows sealed tight. Even then the dirt bowl raised by the machines seeped in and descended on their desks and drawings in fine, brown dust. He held one hand over his ear to try and drown out the noise.

'You do? Sure, 4.30 pm Thursday, suits me fine.'

He turned back to his desk and was about to put the phone down when he saw McQueen, the sour-faced supervisor nosing around. He kept the phone pressed to his ear listening to the disconnected tone, waiting for the clip of McQueen's heels on the wooden floorboards as he patrolled the office.

'Yeah… the rear calliper… that's it.'

He leaned over his desk and ran his finger along the white trace of the brake assembly etched into the blue cobalt of the drawing and waited until McQueen had passed before replacing the phone on its cradle.

*

The afternoon of his appointment he took the bus from the Global Brakes plant in Stratford to downtown Bridgeport. Traffic was snarled up the whole trip. When he reached the city limits the Pequannock River bridge was up. The bus joined a line of trucks and slow moving cars approaching the bridge barrier and juddered to a stop. Through the front screen he watched the bridge deck swing upright into the vertical and lock into place. The driver pushed back his cap, stretched his legs and rested them on the dash. He shrugged his shoulders and mouthed 'Sorry folks' into his rear-view. Miller settled down for the wait until the river traffic had cleared beneath them.

In front of Miller a passenger in mechanic's overalls muttered, 'Aw man, now we goin' to be late.' He leaned round holding an unlit cigarette.

'Got a light?'

Miller dug into his pocket and held out a half-used book of matches. The passenger studied it. On the red cover was a cartoon butler holding out a tray of drinks promoting *Sir MiLord's Tavern, 2100 Superior, Cleveland OH*. He lit his smoke and turned round to Miller.

'You from up there?'

'Yeah, a while back.'

'What brings you down here?'

'You know, the usual, work.'

'D'you go back much?'

'Not if I can help it.'

The passenger held the matches out between his oily fingers.

'Keep 'em.'

'Thanks bud.'

He swept his hand across the steamed-up bus window and looked down on the river where a dredger was working. Its gap-toothed buckets stripped the sediment from the riverbed and disgorged it in a spew of water into a barge tethered alongside. A tug was waiting to tow the barge far out into Long Island Sound where it would unload. A couple of deckhands signaled for the dredging to stop. The whole machine bucked and heaved in the water while they huddled over something dragged up from the riverbed. They prodded it with a boathook, shook their heads and then turned back to their deck work. Who knew what kind of things were washed downstream? Or drifted in on the tide. He had some hunches. In Long Island Sound? Mostly things people wanted rid of: good and permanent. The chain buckets clanked round again and the dredger made its way further downstream, a muddy wake stretching out from its stern. The bridge signals stopped flashing, the drawbridge was lowered and the driver crunched the gears to get the bus going.

Miller stepped off at the corner of Main and Stratford. It was only a couple of blocks to the Institute's office so he browsed the storefronts, stopping at Ace Electricals. The four bucks would just about cover a new radio. He liked the look of the six transistor Zenith in white plastic with a chrome finish that was rotating on a display stand in the centre of the window surrounded by radiograms and television sets. On the other side, a salesman had him in his sights. He was making it look like he was dusting a display, but Miller could see he was sizing him up, revving up his sales pitch. Miller waited for the Zenith to come back round to his side. 'Yes sir, you are a discriminating purchaser if I may say so... This is the all American radio, the Cadillac of transistors... six, yes six, pots of power in this little beauty...' He'd come by later when he had the four bucks.

The Institute of Memory Research was sandwiched between

a menswear store and a jewellers. As Miller pulled open the heavy brass-handled door, a woman hurried towards him from the far end of the hall. She had on a pale blue wool coat that almost reached to her ankles and beetle black shoes with matching black gloves, like her hands and feet had been dipped in ink. She was muttering. It sounded like some kind of rhyme, except it didn't.

'Blue: fox, hat, door, lake. No! Wrong. Here it comes... zapf! Low: dollar, necklace, moon, paint. No! Wrong...'

She brushed right up against him, didn't seem to notice he was there and went straight out the door, which he held open.

'Geez, lady! Where's the fire?'

As she passed, she left a trail of lavender scent and he noticed, underneath the dusting of face powder, she was burning, bright red. Then she was out in the street, took a quick turn left and was gone. He shook his head.

Miller read through the entries on the building register but couldn't see one for the Institute of Applied Memory Research. Instead, there was a notice pinned to the wall inside the doorway.

```
Institute of Applied Memory Research
Please proceed to room B1 in the basement
              Thank you
```

He took the narrow stairway at the end of the hall that led down to the basement. Room B1 was at the end of a corridor lit by a dim overhead light, with a strip of worn carpet running up the middle. There was a stack of cardboard boxes outside the door addressed to AMOS DENTAL LAB with 'return to sender' scrawled across them. Miller hesitated at the door.

He could hear a murmur of conversation. If he wanted to change his mind, he could just walk out now. There was nobody around. It wasn't much of a set up for an Institute: a poky basement, a shabby office building, not even a regular sign – like they didn't plan on being around for long, or didn't want people to know what they were up to.

'C'mon, quit stalling. Four bucks is four bucks.' He rang the bell and went in.

The first thing he noticed was the heat pumping from the industrial-sized radiator that could have fed the entire building. The room had green-coloured walls and scuffed brown linoleum on the floor. A ceiling fan was turning in slow circles, just enough to keep the stuffy air moving. Both the room's windows looked out on the brick-walled alley that ran along the rear of the building. One had bars on the outside and a half drawn curtain. The other, more like a small air grille, high up on the wall was open a fraction. The only furniture was a metal office desk with some books on it and a couple of chairs. Beside the desk was a door marked

STRICTLY PRIVATE

and fixed to the wall was a large, clean mirror.

The two men sitting in the room stopped talking as Miller came in. The one dressed in a blue business suit, too tight for him, with his collar twisted and his tie pulled squint like someone had tugged at it, folded up some papers and put them away in a leather briefcase by his ankles. The other one picked up a clipboard and stood.

'Ah, you'll be…' consulting his clipboard, 'Mr Miller. I'm Hoffman from the Institute, the instructor for this experiment.'

He was tall, with hunched-up shoulders and hair like strands of thin grey wire. He was wearing a technician's coat which reached to his knees, with the sleeves rolled up to the wrists and the coat was too big or he was just bones inside it. Miller had shown up in his work suit, which was frayed around the cuffs from leaning over his drawing board and his shoes were layered with factory dust.

'Pleased to make your acquaintance, sir.' Miller advanced into the office.

'Mr Miller, this is Mr McMurphy, who has also volunteered to work with us.'

'Pleased to make your acquaintance, Mr McMurphy.'

'Good to meet you too, Miller.'

Miller took a seat beside McMurphy while Hoffman went over to the desk, picked up a large book and turned towards them holding the book open like he was about to begin a lesson.

'Gentlemen, thank you for agreeing to participate in this important research. Before we begin I would like to refer to some research on the role of punishment in learning. Authorities such as Wolff and Falke offer diverse perspectives...'

Miller was not really following Hoffman's spiel; he was taking in the contents of the room. The far end had been partitioned off to make a small office with opaque glass panels set into the wall. Pushed up against the outside of the small office was a plain wooden table and a chair. On the table there was an intercom and a large, silver-coloured piece of electrical equipment with an array of dials, switches and cables. It looked like it would drain most of the juice from the Bridgeport power plant.

Hoffman was still talking. 'For example, how does the frequency or intensity of punishment affect retention? There are no definitive answers to many of the key questions such as what kind of punishment has most effect on adults...'

Miller picked up a background buzz, like a low vibration from a power line. The warning on it DANGER ELECTRICITY was not something you needed on a radio. Maybe it was some kind of transmitter, the kind that pumped out the watts from the WADL-777 towers down by the shore.

'Gentlemen, what do you think? Is pain important for what we remember?'

Hoffman looked at them both and closed the book with a snap. McMurphy shrugged his shoulders. Miller did the same. It was not something he had thought about, but you only put your hand on the hot stove once so he reckoned it would be.

'The aim of the experiment is to find out what effect punishment will have on memory retention using this machine.' Hoffman crossed the room and stood beside the table with the electrical apparatus on it. 'The Newton Instruments

Shock Generator.' He beckoned to them to come over. Miller picked up the background buzz again and his eye traced the run of cable snaking from the Newton machine through a duct into the small office. Hoffman carried on. 'I have assigned each of you a role as follows. Mr McMurphy, you will be the learner. Mr Miller, you will be the teacher.'

'Fine by me,' McMurphy said, tucking in his loose shirt.

'And me,' Miller said, not sure what choice he had. He reached for his smokes and started to shake one out when Hoffman held up his hand.

'Would you mind not smoking, Mr Miller?'

'Sure, I guess I can hold out.' He shoved the pack down into his pocket.

'Excellent. Let's begin. Teacher please help me prepare the learner.'

Miller followed Hoffman into the small office. Inside there was a table with a second intercom on it and a swivel chair. McMurphy came in, placed his briefcase under the table, took off his jacket, slung it across the back of the chair and sat down.

'I guess these are for me.' He undid his shirt cuffs, rolled them back and placed his wrists in a pair of restraints attached to the chair's worn leather arm rests.

'Teacher, please fasten the straps.

UNIVERSITY OF NEW ENGLAND:
DEPARTMENT OF PSYCHOLOGY

Record of Experiment 5,
Bridgeport, 22nd October 1962

Subject: Miller, Johnny
Experiment commences at 16.37

The subject is a twenty seven year old draftsman
employed at a large manufacturer of brake products
in Fairport, Con. He has a mild manner, referring
to the instructor as 'sir'. He seems fascinated by
the Newton machine, and pays more attention to it
than the Instructor's introductory talk.

The subject accepts his role as 'teacher', and
McMurphy's role as 'learner', without question.
He listens as the Instructor informs the learner he
will be receiving electric shocks from the teacher
and again raises no objection. As they prepare the
learner the following exchange takes place:

Teacher: (Fingering the restraints) Why do we need
to strap him in?
Instructor: (Checking the restraints for
tightness) This is to prevent any unnecessary
movement when the punishment is applied.
Teacher: (Concerned) Are these electric shocks
safe?
Instructor: (Impatient to proceed) Yes of course.
The electrode paste provides a perfect contact and
although the punishment can be extremely painful,
there is no permanent damage.
Teacher: (Concerned) I don't know much about
electricity…it's not something you fool round
with. I've seen…You can burn someone real bad…
Instructor: (Dismissive) I can assure you the
machine has been fully tested. The experiment is
quite safe. The Institute is responsible for the
conduct of the experiment.
DD

Hoffman stopped halfway out the door. 'Learner, is there anything you want to mention before we commence the experiment?'

'No... I guess I'm OK... Well just one thing... I am feeling a bit breathless.' McMurphy tapped at the intercom button. 'Maybe I'm just anxious?'

'Yes I am sure that's what it is.' Hoffman turned to Miller. 'He's ready. Let's begin.'

Miller touched the surface of the shock generator as he passed and detected a faint electrical tingle in his fingertips. He took off his jacket and sat down. Hoffman was hovering behind him, just like McQueen the supervisor surveying a drawing he was working on before he found what it was he didn't like. The collar of his shirt was chafing and he ran his finger around the inside trying to ease it. He twisted round trying to see what Hoffman was up to.

'Teacher, here are your instructions.' Hoffman's skinny wrist poked from his cuff as he pointed out the switches but did not touch them. 'You will use these to administer punishments to the learner.'

Miller studied the bank of switches ranging from SLIGHT SHOCK 15v to DANGER: SEVERE SHOCK 450v then three additional switches marked XXX.

'First you will read the learner a list of word pairs. Once he has memorised them you will test him to see which ones he remembers.' Hoffman handed him two closely typed pages. Miller read the first line:

```
DEEP lake; FAST river; BLACK curtain; WHITE horse.
```

This was what the beetle woman was blabbering about. Had she been on this side doing the teaching? Or on the other side taking the shocks?

Hoffman continued. 'Each wrong answer the learner gives you will administer the punishment. You will move along the board increasing the voltage level each time.'

Miller leaned back, hands behind his head. 'So, this is what's goin' to teach him not to make mistakes, yeah?'

'The aim is to find out how the punishment improves his learning.'

'I got to tell you, sir, we could use a few of these machines out where I work. We got some real dimwits in the print room who could do with some volts for openers.'

Hoffman sniffed. He uncoiled a cable with an electrode attached to it from the side of the shock generator. 'Will you roll up your sleeve please?'

'Well, isn't McMurphy the one that gets 'em? I'm the Teacher, right?'

'Yes, but we think it is important you feel the effects before you administer the punishment to the learner.' Hoffman began squeezing electrode paste from the tube. Miller rolled up one sleeve and held out his arm. Hoffman smeared on a worm of paste, pressed down the electrode then flicked the switch for 45 volts.

Miller felt a deep jolt. A day in summer. Sun slanting through slats in the loose planks. The oil-stained cement floor, the cloying smell of rubber and gasoline. The pile of corroding batteries in the far corner of the shed where his brother fixed up neighbours' cars and bikes. The knot of other boys, prodding him forwards.

'Go on! Grab 'em or you're a yellowbelly!'

'No I ain't… Give it to me.'

Then he was gripping the stripped cables twisted round the lead terminals and bringing the frayed ends together. The spark jumped the gap and the garage erupted in shouts. Then his brother was there and Miller's hands were up trying to shield his eyes from the shock of sudden light. Miller half choked back a shout.

'Turn it off!'

Hoffman peered down at him.

'That's the test shock complete, Mr Miller. I take it you are OK to carry on?'

Miller nodded his head. 'Yeah… it just seemed… well,

more than I thought.' He rubbed at the dull ache that persisted in his arm. Hoffman reset the switch and coiled the cable. Then he reached into his coat, took out a white cloth and cleaned his hands. Miller wiped the paste residue from his hands on the tops of his work pants. Hoffman returned to the desk and sat down. 'Teacher, please begin the test.'

UNIVERSITY OF NEW ENGLAND:
DEPARTMENT OF PSYCHOLOGY

Record of Experiment 5,
Bridgeport, 22nd October 1962

Subject: Miller, Johnny
16.57

At the 75v level when the learner gives his first audible feedback — a grunt — the subject stiffens slightly in the chair and the following exchange takes place:

Teacher: (Turning round) Did you hear that?
Instructor: (Barely raising his head from his notes) Please continue teacher.
Teacher: (Looking up towards the glass) Hey McMurphy, is everything OK in there?
Instructor: (Raising his voice) The experiment requires that you continue. Go on with the next question please.
Teacher: (Hesitant) OK McMurphy… here we go again.

At this stage the subject is still compliant, even though the instructor is oblivious to the learner's complaints. He shows growing signs of discomfort at the learner's protests although he continues to administer what he believes are increasing levels of shock.
DD

Miller leaned forward and asked McMurphy the next word pair. He was maybe a dozen questions into the test and he was already giving him over 100 volts. He couldn't understand why McMurphy was so slow on the uptake. While he waited for the answer he glanced out the window to his left. High on the wall on the building opposite steam vented from an open exhaust. He felt like he was sitting right beneath it. He reached into his pocket for his smokes. Then he remembered what Hoffman had said and swivelled round.

'Any chance of turning this thing up? I'm suffocatin' here.' Miller gestured towards the sluggish ceiling fan with his thumb.

Hoffman looked over at him and without shifting his gaze made a mark on his notes. 'Teacher, the fan appears to be functioning to me.' Miller ran his finger around the inside of his collar again, tried to ease it away where it was sticking to his neck then turned his back on Hoffman.

'Just my opinion but you need to speak to whoever runs this goddam building and get some maintenance done.'

'Please continue, teacher.'

McMurphy's answer crackled over the intercom. 'Apple.'

Miller gripped the intercom with both hands.

'Wrong! 'Ink'… McMurphy concentrate will you… You've got a whole bunch more here to get through and you're up to 125 volts already.' He reached for the switch, held his finger there, shaking, then pressed down hard. McMurphy yelped. His hollering was getting on Miller's nerves. He needed to make McMurphy understand. 'You keep gettin' the shocks because you're makin' so many damn mistakes!'

He was feeling it was McMurphy's fault.

It was like McMurphy was making him do it.

'OK McMurphy. Next word. 'Bag'… Answer please.'

Another wrong answer. Miller flicked the 150v switch. This time it was different. Miller strained to hear what McMurphy said.

'I don't… want to… go on.'

Miller wasn't sure if he'd heard him right. He turned to Hoffman.

'I think he said he's through. What do I do now?'

UNIVERSITY OF NEW ENGLAND:
DEPARTMENT OF PSYCHOLOGY

Record of Experiment 5,
Bridgeport, 22nd October 1962

Subject: Miller, Johnny
17.07

The subject complains about the experimental
conditions and seems about to challenge the
instructor's authority. He shows visible signs of
stress and is increasingly frustrated with the
learner's mistakes, seeing him as responsible in
some way for his own conduct.

At the crucial 150v level the conflict between the
instructor's demands and the subject's concern for
the learner intensifies. The subject faces a key
moment of decision. Will he remain compliant or
will he take responsibility for his own actions?

Instructor: (Neutral tone) Please continue.
Teacher: (Facing the instructor) Did you hear him?
He said he wants to stop.
Instructor: (Looking up from his notes) The
experiment requires that you continue.
Teacher: (Raising his voice) You heard him before.
He said he was breathless. What if his heart gives
out?
Instructor: (Voice quavering) It is essential you
continue. The punishments may be painful but there
is no lasting effect.
Teacher: (Rising from his seat and looking through
the glass). Hey McMurphy — you OK in there?
DD

Miller sat down again, his eyes boring into the shock generator, penetrating its metal skin, right through it to its veins of copper wire and its glowing silvered valves. The voltmeter needle quivered like a twitching nerve. He pressed his hands to his temples.

'Please continue, teacher.'

'The next word is 'Cool – breeze, water, day, light.' Answer please...'

McMurpy's answer was hoarse and tinny. 'Breeze...'

'Naw... the answer is 'water'... cool water.'

He checked with Hoffman again.

'You think I should keep givin' him the shocks even though he says to quit?'

'That's correct, teacher, please administer the punishment.'

Miller rubbed at his arm. He swivelled round. 'I can't treat him like he's a dumb animal in a cage.' Hoffman, head bowed over his notes, straightened up. His eyes were grey like molten lead.

'Do you want to be responsible for abandoning the experiment? Please administer the punishment.'

Miller shook his head. 'He says he wants to stop. You say go ahead. I don't know... this don't seem right to me.' He reached for the 175v switch held his hand over it and pressed down.

The warning light glowed and the generator buzzed as the power engaged. The voltmeter snapped to the right like a sprung trap as the current discharged and he was sure he heard McMurphy buck in the chair again as the power surged through him.

'No!... Please!... Stop!'

UNIVERSITY OF NEW ENGLAND:
DEPARTMENT OF PSYCHOLOGY

Record of Experiment 5,
Bridgeport, 22nd October 1962

Subject: Miller, Johnny
17.14

Teacher: (Angry) This ~~not~~ can't go on.
Instructor: (Strict) You have no choice… Continue…
Ask the next question.
Teacher: (Angry) Of course I have choice! You
heard him — he ~~wants~~ says to stop. If you want it,
you do it. (Rising from his seat) I'm going in…
Instructor: (Pleading) Please don't Mr Miller!
(Looking towards mirror) Professor, I will have to
terminate the experiment.

Expmnt ends 17.17.
DD

Miller heard Hoffman's 'Please don't' as he shoved the chair back so fast it tipped. A quick look through the glass. Was that McMurphy slumped over? Hoffman was up waving at the mirror.

Miller yanked open the door and stumbled into the office: it was like he had prised open the lid on something meant to stay shut.

McMurphy was on his knees, twisting round to see who it was. 'Miller?'

It didn't add up. The empty chair. The spilt coffee. The copy of *Billboard* open on the table. The tape player. Then McMurphy was huffing and hauling himself upright, gripping a power chord in one hand.

'I can explain…'

'Cut the static, McMurphy.' He'd caught him, but what at? He pulled at the restraints on the chair. They seemed secure enough when he tied him in. Nobody else had been in the room so the chair had some kind of hidden release. Where was McMurphy getting his instructions from? Telephone maybe? He studied the ceiling. No sign of a line. No handset either. McMurphy stood on the far side of the table, spooling tape on a player. Miller took out a smoke and lit it.

'So that's where the sound effects were comin' from, yeah?'

McMurphy nodded, placing the tape in a cardboard sleeve.

'So, while I'm out there stewin' over how much juice I'm givin' you, you're in here, workin' the player, maybe gettin' instructions, cup of coffee and a magazine when you need a break… is that it?' He blew smoke in McMurphy's direction.

'You're not the only stewing in here…' McMurphy wiped a hand across his brow. 'But this isn't how it usually goes.'

'You mean the fast one you and Hoffman are pulling?'

'It's not a put up job, not the way you think.' McMurphy was struggling into his jacket, damp stains showing on his shirt underarms. 'Anyway, the professor will take you through it.'

Miller took a last draw from his cigarette and stubbed it out in the coffee cup.

'Wait up bud.' He held up his hand in front of McMurphy's chest. 'What 'professor' are you talkin' about?'

'He means me, Mr Miller.'

Miller swung round. The professor was standing in the doorway, arms crossed over his mustard turtleneck, tugging at his wispy beard. He was studying Miller from behind dark-rimmed spectacles, eyes intense black like carbon.

'So you're the one responsible for this memory test baloney?'

'Yes, I'm Don Davidson and this is my set up, or what's left of it.' He glanced around the room. 'Please, come with me. We have a great deal to talk about Mr Miller.'

Miller glanced at McMurphy who was stowing the tape player in his briefcase then followed the professor to the desk where they sat down. The professor called Hoffman over.

'Abe, could you bring my notes please.' Hoffman opened the door marked STRICTLY PRIVATE.

'You been watchin' this whole thing from in there?'

'Yes, a necessary subterfuge I'm afraid.' Hoffman returned and handed the professor his typed notes. 'Thank you, Abe. Please bring a chair and join us.' Hoffman wheeled out the chair that McMurphy had sat in. Its castors squeaked on the brown linoleum floor. He pulled it up beside Miller and sat legs stretched out, arms resting on the loose restraints, occasionally rubbing his hands together like he had cleaned them well.

UNIVERSITY OF NEW ENGLAND:
DEPARTMENT OF PSYCHOLOGY

Record of Experiment 5,
Bridgeport, 22nd October 1962

Subject: Miller, Johnny
Review of experiment

Professor: Well, Mr Miller I feel we have all
learned a great deal today. I think you know
that the leaner was quite unharmed. I think you
also realize that, in fact, no shocks were given
at all. Quite often this comes as a surprise to
our subjects. Now as to the real purpose of our
experiment…
Teacher: I reckon it's no memory test.
Professor: Well you are correct of course.
The real purpose of the experiment was to see how
far you would follow Hoffman's orders.
Teacher: So this whole set up… just to see if I'd
follow his orders?
Professor: We need to go to these lengths…
Teacher: The one way mirror… the actor… the bogus
machine… I feel like I've been suckered…
Professor: Please Mr Miller, I need to make sure
you understand…
Miller: …I don't think I need to stick around.
Professor: I…
Teacher: You can keep the four bucks. I reckon the
bills are fake.
Professor: Please Mr Miller… you will receive a
report… you acted with great courage…
DD
(NB Review Hoffman's role in the experiment)

Miller came out of the drugstore with a fresh pack of Camels tucked into his pocket. The wind was picking up, plucking at the utility cables that stretched in a wire cage above the city streets. He walked along the sidewalk holding his collar pinched tight at the neck against a serrated edge of sleety rain until he came to the Kandy Korner diner. He paused to light a smoke in the entrance and went inside.

He stood and soaked up the heat and the glare radiating off the metal surfaces and breathed in the fug of hot fat. Customers perched on high stools, with their elbows resting on the counter top, levering up their plates of food and draining down their mugs of steaming coffee. On the other side of the counter, the cooks in their greasy whites sweated over the sizzling grill, calling out the orders in turn.

'Steak 'n' eggs comin' right up!' and 'Kelly, you're on!'

He slid into a red leatherette booth in the far corner. A waitress with a stacked beehive of blonde hair, crisp as a nurse in her starched uniform, came over to him, pot of coffee in one hand and a mug with two Ks stamped on it in the other.

'You sure do look like a man who needs a strong cup of coffee.'

He nodded. 'Yeah, unless you got anything stronger.'

'Not the last time I looked.' She set the mug down in front of him. 'Shout when you want a refill, hon.' She smiled and turned away then began fussing around another customer who had just come in from outside and was peeling off his olive green gabardine.

Miller reached for the cream and trickled it into his coffee, watching the pattern of white bomblets fall on the dark brown surface. The customer who had just come in stood at the side of the booth.

'Do you mind if I take the load off my feet?' he said.

Miller looked up. 'What you doin' here, McMurphy?' His face was flushed and he was breathing hard. He squeezed his belly along the edge of the table and into the booth, laid his gabardine on the seat beside him then loosened off his tie.

'I come in here most days when we're through.' He took out a large purple handkerchief and wiped it across his brow. 'You showed me a clean pair of heels coming down here. I hung around in the corridor 'til you left the building. Almost lost you when you came out of the drugstore.'

Miller looked across towards the entrance.

'Naw, it's just me. I left Hoffman and Davidson having their chin wag.'

The blonde waitress stood smiling beside the table with a coffee that she set down in front of McMurphy.

'Usual, Murph?'

'Thanks, Kelly.'

She reached up into her hair do and extracted a pen, gave the tip a quick, ready for business lick, flipped open her order book and scribbled.

'Be right back with the pie.' McMurphy grinned after her.

'You and the rest of the phonies at the Institute must work up a real hearty appetite.' Miller reached past him and stubbed out his smoke. A curl of smoke drifted up from the smouldering cigarette end. McMurphy fanned it away. 'My memory must be getting bad. Why did you say you followed me here?'

'There was something I was wondering about.' The waitress returned and set a bowl of pie with a thick, toasted meringue crust in front of McMurphy. He looked up at her and smiled then poked at the pie with a spoon until it caved in and lemon filling spilled out.

'Yeah? Well there's a bunch of things I'm wonderin' about. Let's start with the fast one you and your phony friends are pullin'.'

McMurphy took a spoonful of pie, reached for a napkin and wiped some yellow stickiness away from his mouth. His eyes hardened. 'Like I told you. It's not a have-on and I'm not a phony, OK. I am an actor, Miller. Small stuff, bit parts, voiceovers. Some radio work for WADL. No big breaks. No Hollywood producers knocking on my door and no starlets neither. I have to take what I can get.' He jabbed his spoon into hard-baked base. 'Beggars can't be choosers in this game.'

'Actor huh? That crybaby routine of yours,' Miller took a swig of his coffee. 'That's a real tear jerker.'

'I don't write the lines; I just read them. If you'd hung around you'd have heard the Professor explain it. But you legged it out of there like…'

'Yeah, well I couldn't stomach any more of his baloney. And Hoffman was making me jumpy. I knew I shouldn't have trusted him, shouldn't have trusted any of it.' He spun his pack of Camels around on the shiny tabletop.

McMurphy put down his spoon, wiped his mouth and straightened his tie. He picked up the Camels and began a spiel, like he'd landed a part in a tobacco promotion.

'More doctors smoke Camels than any other brand.'

He took a long drag from an imaginary cigarette and rolled it around in his fingers. 'He's a smiling, grey-haired guy, with a healthy tan from all the time he's spent on the golf course, stethoscope dangling from his neck, relaxing with a smoke after a long, hard day on the examination couch.' McMurphy took another drag and sniffed. 'Dress some guy up in a white coat, say he's a doc, to Joe Public he is a doc.' He stubbed out the invisible smoke. 'And if you can't trust a doc, Miller, who can you trust?' He placed the pack on the table. 'Same with Davidson's routine, except instead of a doc it's a scientist.

Over by the counter two of the waitresses were swaying to a song playing over the radio. McMurphy picked up the beat and tapped his fingers on the tabletop. Hoffman had looked the part in his technician's get up, calling the shots, telling him to ramp it up, saying the shocks were safe. He was the one in charge so Miller went along with what he said.

'Maybe I should have ignored your hollerin' and kept goin' like Hoffman said. Left you in there, strapped up to Old Sparky. Taken the four bucks and walked.'

'A lot of folks just want to be told what to do.'

'Yeah, well if it's about tellin' folks what to do, the professor could've saved himself the trouble and come on up to

Global Brakes. McQueen could teach him a few tricks: crackin' the whip's his speciality.'

'Do you remember the woman took the test before you came in? Respectable looking, school secretary.'

Miller nodded, 'Yeah I remember her.'

'What do you think happens?'

He pictured her again, scuttling down the hallway towards him dressed up in black gloves and shoes, fiery red under the face powder. 'I reckons she gives up, can't take your hollerin'.'

McMurphy shook his head. 'We get to "I can't go on" and she turns up the juice. Keeps going 'til I've croaked as far as she knows. Davidson sits her down afterwards. 'Tell me Miss Doberman, were you at all concerned for Mr McMurphy's welfare?' She looks like she's taken a shot of vinegar and says, 'I did just what you wanted, Professor.' She went right to the end of the board, Miller. Would have kept on going if Hoffman hadn't stopped her. Right to the end of the board.'

Miller fingered the spot on his arm where the electrode had made contact.

'I guess she was tryin' to get out of Hoffman's coils, same as me.'

'Yeah, except you didn't keep giving me the juice after I'd clammed up. That's the big difference. Most give up when I start hollering. But nobody, not 'til now,' he played a drum roll on the table top, 'comes riding to the rescue like the goddam 7th Cavalry.' He stopped drumming and leaned forward, holding his hands open. 'What was going on Miller? Why'd you burst in like that?'

Miller looked out the window. He put his hand up to his neck. Hoffman had put him in a chokehold. If you struggled against it, you cut off your own air. But you needed to breathe. It was the same with McQueen strutting round the drawing office like he was king of the roost. Some guy's always standing over you calling the shots. Some poor sap's always jumping through hoops.

He looked out at Main Street.

'I wasn't burstin' in…'

He watched a line of sleet slide down the window.

'I was breakin' out.'

McMurphy inspected the empty dish in front of him then pushed it away. The waitress was hovering close by and reached over to retrieve it. From behind the counter one of the cooks called out.

'Hey, hush up folks, there's a bulletin coming.'

The waitress paused beside the table. Miller tapped out a cigarette from his pack and lit it. Behind the counter someone was adjusting the radio, getting the aerial positioning right. The announcer's voice faded, then grew louder.

'We are interrupting our programme for a presidential news bulletin live from the White House.' Miller twisted round, tuning in to the word coming down the wire.

Kennedy's voice projected into the diner. 'Good evening, my fellow citizens. This Government has, as promised, maintained the closest surveillance of the Soviet military build-up on the island of Cuba…'

Miller gripped the tabletop. He let out a low whistle. Cuba – they were going to fight the Russians over goddam Cuba. The couple in the next booth turned to each other and the woman asked, 'What's happening? Does anyone know what's happening?' Someone at the counter replied without turning, 'Now those Commies are going to gets what's comin' to 'em. That's what.' His buddy, sitting alongside, tapped his agreement on the counter. Miller reached for his cigarette. It had burned away to ash.

The waitress shook her head and began clearing tables again, muffling the noise of dishes with her apron. McMurphy stretched across the table for the smokes. Miller fished in his pocket for some matches and slid them over. McMurphy lit up and stared outside.

'Hear it?' McMurphy blew a cloud of smoke that drifted along the window.

Miller listened. He heard the tic of the stovetop as it cooled, the hum of compressors in the fridges, the rumble of traffic, his own heartbeat like a hammer on metal. He was waiting for some kind of signal coming that it had started.

'I don't hear no jets if that's what you mean. What're you hearing?'

McMurphy drew hard on the cigarette.

'Prayers,' he exhaled.

Miller looked around the diner. People were waiting for someone to make a move, like that moment at the end of a funeral when everyone wants to leave but no one gets up to go. He couldn't see any hands clasped. Didn't hear anyone calling, 'Oh Lord, where art thou?'

'Who's prayin?'

McMurphy took a deep breath.

'Out there, under the Kansas cornfields, the boys in the concrete bunkers down on their knees, begging sweet Jesus for forgiveness after they've pressed the button that brings fiery hell raining down on all of us.'

Miller looked outside. Storefront signs were still lit. Traffic was moving. The stoplight swayed above the intersection. The foundries at Global Brakes would still be blazing. Inside the diner, they were serving again.

'The machine's up and running, McMurphy. Nothin' we can do to stop it.'

McMurphy was hunched up in the corner of the booth, head pressed against the glass. He looked up.

'Get in its way, Miller, it'll just roll over you.' Then McMurphy turned and stared out the window again, still listening.

Miller stood up, shook out a couple of smokes and left them lined up in a snug silo on the table.

*

Back on Main Street Miller retraced his steps to the Pequannock. He needed to feel the breeze that was blowing in from the Sound.

Traffic drummed across the steel deck of the bridge. He leaned up against the concrete parapet and listened to the river's oily slop against the bridge's iron supports. He straightened up and lit a cigarette, filling his lungs with smoke and sulphurous, salty river air.

There was a light on in the operator's cabin, and he could see a figure moving about inside. The window rattled open.

'Hey bud!'

'Yeah?'

'Not a jumper are you?'

Miller reckoned there'd be easier ways.

'Naw, just getting some air.' Miller gestured with his smoke.

'If you're ever considerin' it, save yourself the drop. Take a bath. Enough chemicals goin' down there to sluice out every john in Bridgeport.' The operator was still laughing as the window slammed shut.

Miller was surrounded by shouts from deckhands and stevedores working the piers below him. The air vibrated with revving motors and pulsing diesels. He gripped the parapet of the bridge, muscles taut as hawsers and looked across the river's inky surface towards the power plant out on the point. Its grey concrete shell, vast as a bunker, was studded with lights. The fields of coal around it smouldered orange under the glare of its arc lamps. The hum of the generators buried deep inside the building radiated out to him. He looked up. Stretching through the cables that criss-crossed the sky above him, the electrifying current flowed.

STALEMATE

Simon Griffiths

During the first few days the media drew a complete blank, not a single image of the tsunami. Henry thought it disgraceful. A twenty-four hour news cycle, fibre-optic cable spanning the globe, a digital camera in every other back pocket, and yet still the twenty-first century found itself swallowed by this hole of not-knowing.

He spent the day flicking between different news programs, scouring for developments. His back and hips ached. He'd barely moved from his comfy chair, but decided the pain was irrelevant. He wanted to concentrate on the gaping lack of information. There were the most awful scenes, it had the potential of a riveting narrative, and he was finding it, by far, the most effective distraction.

It was a vacuum into which his mind rushed, a pressure differential seeking balance. Like the media, his thoughts ran with the snippets of detail, spinning out whole worlds of explanation.

The death toll was estimated at twenty-three thousand. He wanted to do something to help, maybe donate money to a charity. But it was hard to decide which one. Some of them would no doubt waste the bulk of it on administration.

All the channels had reporters on location, interviews with shell-shocked tourists, and footage of the homeless, emaciated locals, many of them knelt in prayer. Henry scoffed and railed. It was a reflex. A familiar, and, as he himself acknowledged, not entirely original refrain. 'What kind of a god… ?'

At one point his curses brought on a coughing fit. His whole body shook and he had to lean forward. He put a hand to his chest and with the other he fumbled on his little wheeled dining table, searching for the emergency buzzer.

Fortunately, the next report focused on the fact that there'd been no early warnings. The appropriate technology would've saved many lives. Experts were calling for advanced systems to be put in place. Henry nodded in agreement. As abruptly as it began, his coughing died down. He caught his breath. He'd had worse. His hand let the buzzer slide back onto the table. No need to call the care staff.

In short, the media could do aftermath by the bucketful. But of the event itself, nothing. That was until the fourth day. When the early evening news held out a promise. The first footage.

Sean, one of the male carers, rapped on Henry's door.

'Finished your dinner?'

'Have you finished?' Henry tutted, unsure whether to be more annoyed by the interruption or Sean's grammar.

'Sorry?' Sean came in, stood in front of the bulky television and looked down at Henry's plate. The Shepherd's Pie was rearranged.

'Still not hungry?'

'I've had enough.'

'But you've hardly touched it, look at all that lovely mince, it's your favourite.'

'I'm trying to watch this.' Henry gestured to the television.

Sean stepped aside, allowing Henry to focus on the news reporter, who spoke, in Queen's English, over the video.

'This was the moment when the tsunami struck the centre of Banda Aceh. The man behind the camera risks his life to film the raging torrent, ten feet high, as it sweeps passed him.'

Dirty black water surged down the main street, thick and viscous like wave upon wave of magma. It carried with it furniture, bric-a-brac, masses of shattered wood, a whole tree, its branches and leaves aloft. An Indonesia woman clambered to safety and the camera cut to a convergence of vans and cars, barging and banging as the water swept them around a junction.

Sean knelt down beside Henry, picked up the fork and loaded it with mince and mash. 'Come on, try just a little bit?'

'No.'

'You need to keep your strength up.' Sean wavered the fork in front of Henry.

'I don't need help. But you just carry on. Never mind what I say.'

'Alright mate, have it your way.' Sean put the fork down and leant back.

The news report had cut to what was obviously a holiday video. A subtitled, German tourist commented on how strange it was, the tide had gone out really fast and all the boats were beached. The next shot showed the tide coming back. Really fast. On the horizon a huge wave chewed up two boats, the digicam was at maximum zoom, straining to capture the action. But the tourists just stood on the beach, filming the wave. They commented on how crazy it was, but didn't make a move. The cameraman even said. 'Look, all the Thais are running.'

Sean let out a sigh. 'Henry, what's going on? This is the third day you've not eaten.'

Henry continued staring at the screen, where a blue hotel pool was being overrun by a torrent of white water. It was the same German couple. The voices of the cameraman and his wife were filled with panic.

'Quick, get over here.'

'I can't, not with the children.'

'I'm coming.'

The video cut out and in the studio the anchor noted that the death toll was estimated at sixty thousand.

Henry felt a rush of sadness that he quickly tried to quell. It was no use. He wondered if the German couple had died, if their children had died, and from there he couldn't help but think about his own two friends, who'd definitely died that Boxing Day.

Eddie and Maud. His friends. One death awaited, the other not. Eddie's diagnosis had been terminal. Cancer.

Maud's was unforeseen. A total shock to the home. But not entirely to Henry.

On Boxing Day morning, Sean had walked into Henry's room. His brow was pinched and his upper lip quivered slightly.

Sean knelt down beside him. 'I'm sorry mate, but I've got some bad news, in the night, Maud passed.'

Henry wasn't surprised. He only felt a sense of confirmation. It'd been dark when the dream woke him. He couldn't remember the details. Just that he was filled with dread. And for some reason the certainty of Maud's death.

For the rest of the morning, as news of the tsunami broke, he was terrified by the question that overran his thoughts. How had he known? He considered himself a man of science. It was anathema to everything he believed. That kind of thing just didn't happen. And yet, he had known.

It was Sean's turn to do the morning tea trolley. This was a few days into the new year. Henry's door was ajar and Sean knocked before entering. He held Henry's favourite mug, from which rose a drift of steam. The news was on the TV. Henry was standing at his dresser, rooting through one of the drawers. On top of the dresser sat a chessboard. The pieces were positioned as if a game was still in progress. Henry looked up and rubbed the stubble on his cheek.

'Can't get enough of the news these days, can you?' Sean said.

Henry gave a sshh of reprimand. He moved from the dresser and stood listening, one hand on the back of his comfy chair.

It was a news story about how hardly any animals had been killed by the Tsunami. Interviewees gave accounts of 'strange' animal behaviour, a Park Ranger told how their elephants ran for higher ground an hour beforehand, a man credited his dog with saving their lives: that morning the dog refused to go for his walk along the beach.

The reporter interviewed an animal expert who said that for centuries animals had been credited with possessing a sixth sense.

'Pah, absolute rubbish.' Henry said.

The expert went on to say that humans may have also possessed such an intuitive sense at one time, but that technological progress had rendered it obsolete.

'And where's your proof?' Henry turned to Sean. 'These rent a quote 'experts', I tell you, the money they get paid.'

'Not the sort of thing you hear about everyday though, is it?' Sean said. 'Anyway, you had your wash this morning?'

Henry was back at the dresser, going through the next drawer down. He stopped momentarily, as if digesting Sean's question.

'I can't find my glasses, there's an article I've got to read. Do you know if that Mandy moved them when she tidied up?'

'I can ask her, but I doubt she put them in with your clothes. You want a hand?'

Sean put Henry's mug on the wheeled table and went over to the dresser. He took a quick step back, holding a thumb and forefinger to his nose.

'We really should get you a bath Henry. I can give you a shave too.'

'I don't need any help. If it wasn't for that stupid girl, putting everything in the wrong place.' Henry turned to Sean and slapped his hand down on top of the dresser. The heel of his palm caught the edge of the chessboard launching the carved wooden pieces across the room in a graceful arc. A bishop, a rook, five pawns, two kings and one queen.

Henry glared at Sean and shouted. 'Look what you've made me do.'

To him the board was a testimony. The pieces positioned as they were when Eddie died. Their last unfinished game. Now all of them lay scattered on the floor.

Sean didn't respond, apart from to gather up the chessmen. And with each piece that he placed back on the wrong square, the pitch of Henry's anger rose.

He clenched his fists white. 'You just ignore me then. Always the same bloody story.'

Sean returned to the door, still seemingly oblivious, and Henry felt his anger plummet. What was the point? He slumped down in his chair. Before leaving, Sean reminded him to drink his tea before it went cold. Henry didn't answer. He was lost to his memories of that last game.

As usual he'd set up the chessboard before Eddie's arrival. He was sitting in the lounge, listening out for the booming chatter that marked Eddie being wheeled down the corridor. He was a large and jovial man with a fondness for loud jumpers.

Instead, Sean walked in, came over to the table and said. 'Sorry, but I don't think Eddie's going to make it today.'

'Oh dear, well, what am I supposed to do?'

'There's the papers, or you could go back to your room?'

'Would you care for a game?'

'Afraid I'm too busy mate.'

Henry's expression dropped.

'Can you think of anyone else who could play?'

'Not really... tell you what, let me go and speak to Eddie, see if we can't arrange a change of venue.'

This became the new routine. Each morning Henry made his way up to Eddie's room, where he would be waiting, propped up in bed. What Henry found impressive was that to the end, as the cancer caused his body to crumble and break down around him, Eddie retained the bulk of his mind. He wasn't the opponent of former games, his moves were mainly reactive and defensive, and to keep things going Henry had to resort to the odd blatant sacrifice, but still, Eddie's lucidity was enviable when compared with the unravelling of some residents.

On the whole, Henry had to conclude that cancer was an admirable way to go. What more of a bodily failure than for your own cells to turn against you. He was hoping for the same but had long since decided that for him it'd be the coal dust in his lungs.

In Eddie's case, the stretches of clarity were balanced by a tendency to fall asleep. Sometimes while about to castle, or move a pawn. Their last game stretched out over five days, into Christmas week. Each morning Eddie managed fewer moves. Henry sensed that it was their final game, but he couldn't tell if they'd bring it to a close.

On the Monday Eddie dozed off before even making a move. Henry spent ten minutes watching him breathe, waiting to see if he'd wake up. Nothing happened. There was just Eddie's breath. A broken, rattling inhalation, an extended pause, and a ponderous, wheezing exhalation. In the end, Henry wondered, was this what life came down to, a laboured staccato rhythm that finally ran out of steam?

He shuffled along the corridor, his right knee clicking and his eyes fixed on the carpet's red and black diamond weave. Back in his room he thumped down into his chair. His ankles ached and every muscle was exhausted by the corridor.

The burgundy folder was on his dresser so he didn't stay seated for long. He stood, retrieved it and returned to the chair. If he was going to have a snooze, he needed to get a couple of things down first. Playing chess with Eddie was the closest he'd been to anyone's deathbed. He didn't want to waste the opportunity.

Henry opened the folder and caught the smell of the lined, green graph paper. He always chose the same paper for his little projects. A reminder of what could have been. Of what he'd lost.

On the same graph paper his supervisor, Arthur Raglan, had scrawled illegible notes about the machines and their working order. Arthur Raglan, an older man in his forties who always ribbed Henry for being a coward.

That morning Henry's hands were sticky with oil from the machinery. He grabbed one of the woven cloths they used on the machine floor. It had been washed but its colour was still off grey.

Arthur called him.

Henry wiped his hands as he walked across. The cloth felt waxy against his skin. He flinched. Pain stabbed up his arm.

Arthur laughed, grabbed Henry's wrist and turned it over. 'For God's sake boy, stop squirming. Open your hand.'

A thin twist of metal glinted back, embedded in his palm.

Henry winced and tried to fee himself. Arthur held fast and shouted so everyone could hear. 'Just proves what a yellow-belly you am, bleating over a bit of swarf.'

All the men laughed. And that was when Henry snapped. When he decided he couldn't stand it any more. He'd show Arthur Raglan. He'd sign up that very lunch hour.

His stomach felt hollow. He loved the satisfaction of getting the machines running smoothly. He didn't want to leave that behind. But the army surely needed engineers, so maybe he wouldn't have to give it up.

When he got back to work and declared his news, Arthur laughed in his face.

'You're a fool boy, to be so easily swayed.'

As Eddie was steadily consumed, Henry found himself playing the consummate scientific observer. He was more detached than he expected. Able to watch both the board and Eddie's demise. He thought it might have been the inevitability, the feeling of being forewarned.

In fact, when it came to his objectivity, Henry considered there to have been only one slip. On the Thursday before Christmas, a bishop held in mid-air, Eddie started to sob.

Tears openly streamed down his cheeks as he cried out. 'But Henry, I don't want to die like this.'

Henry felt an urge to reach across the board, to lay his hand upon Eddie's. But if he wasn't comfortable with one grown man crying, he certainly wasn't at ease with two of them holding hands.

He didn't know what to do. He felt disturbed and, without a clear purpose in mind, he stood up. He mumbled an excuse, turned and walked out. He spent the whole of the corridor back trying to ignore the pang in his solar plexus.

People said you came to a care home to see out your final years. To Henry it seemed more that the vast majority of residents came to rush through their last few months. For many, moving from their own home to the care home, whatever the reasons and circumstances, it seemed too traumatic. They didn't cope with the transition.

The shock and bewilderment, everything they knew, and were used to, gone, replaced by this unfamiliar institution with its one biscuit rule and it's four o'clock teatime.

There were those who wondered around looking lost, and others like Milly, one of the home's newest residents, who wore an expression of permanent surprise, as if she'd tried to avoid the place by having one too many facelifts.

Henry remembered first mulling with the idea of a graph. It would cover all of the homes residents, including himself, and plot everyone's descent. At that point he'd been in the home for two years and had noticed the number of new residents who didn't last more than a few months. It seemed exponentially high, but he wanted hard data.

The evidence he gathered was convincing. Many did, in fact, enter the home able to walk to the dining room unaided. But after weeks or months, Henry would often find himself updating their file, having noted the regular offer of a supportive staff arm. Then would come the point where getting down the corridor took too long and the risk of falls became too great.

He would watch them being pushed on the same journey, frail and wheelchair bound, as if some part inside had snapped.

Henry wondered about the manner of his own arrival at this final threshold. If the time came, and he required a wheelchair, he hoped to welcome it with open arms and feet neatly tucked in. There was an incontrovertible objectivity to the failure of the body. A certainty he found reassuring.

The more subjective, and worrying, form of decline was mental. The erosion of the mind. To a man who based his identity on a sense of intellectual superiority, no prospect was more terrifying.

Over the last four years, he'd even made a concerted effort. All the chess games, the dancing, the crosswords and his arrangement with Doctor Crawford, who passed along old copies of Nature and New Scientist.

His research left him in no doubt about the presence of that old dichotomy. The split between mind and body. Foregoing accidents and illness, something would give out. There was always a weak link. Inevitably, one of them would go first. Either the mind or the body.

Over the years Henry's initial graphs had turned into a more private and elaborate study. In a sense, he considered himself the home's registrar of deaths. Observations, notes, charts and theories. The deaths themselves, the causal links, the various lengths of decline, all of them plotted and marked out. Perhaps it was a grim topic, but it gave Henry a certain comfort. If he could foresee the manner of his own demise, if he could spot the signs, that would give him a sense of having mastered the situation.

Eddie was the only person he'd told.

'Henry, that's rather macabre.'

'But it happens to everyone,' Henry said. 'No one can escape their mortality. The only real question is the manner in which you go.'

Death, it felt like an old master that foresaw all the moves.

Victory may have been impossible, but Henry always questioned whether it was plausible to play for a kind of stalemate. It wasn't a matter of cheating death, but more of ensuring it didn't catch you unaware. To see it coming, to face it, that was his idea of a good death.

Henry had first asked, and later insisted. The residents needed a computer with the Internet. He originally settled for dial-up, but events in South-East Asia had exposed its inadequacy. He tapped his knuckles on the desk. He sighed and harrumphed. He alternated between a study of the lounge carpet's red and black diamonds and quick glances at the luminous green bar making its slow advance. It was ridiculous, ten minutes to download a thirty-second video of the tsunami.

He decided the only answer was a campaign to drag the home into the age of broadband. That was the problem with progress. It came ready-mixed with frustration. Once you caught the bug, satisfaction became impossible. The leading edge always ran two steps ahead.

His hip ached. He stood up and shuffled to the other side of the lounge. His gaze snagged on a picture tacked to the wall. It'd been taken by a digital camera and printed on A4 paper. Him and Maud. Face to face. In their Sunday best. Dancing the Foxtrot.

He sat down and let the memory seep back, one element at a time. Her soft, lopsided smile. A flash of her awful teeth, stained and worn, reminding him of stumps running down a beach.

Then a perception he'd dismissed as far too subjective. The music started up and after the first four bars her eyes sizzled with recognition. She hummed the tune. He offered her his hand. She studied it for a second before realising its purpose. Her thin, elongated fingers gripped his firmly. He placed his other hand in the small of her back and she flinched, looking at him quizzically, as if surprised by this invasion of her personal space.

But she was by far the better dancer. Some synapse would flare. The memory would storm back and they'd be off on their Foxtrot come amble around the lounge.

His video had long since finished downloading. But the image of Maud kept coming back to him. That moment of recognition as her memory sparked. He tried to rationalise this impression, but instead found himself silently crying.

If, with Eddie, objectivity was everything, when it came to the addition of Maud's details he found it nigh on impossible to remain detached. And why, he wondered, was that? Why had her death hit him so hard? Surely her suffering was over. She had Alzheimer's.

Her daughter had told him how Maud would never talk about the war, about what she did, except to say that was when she fell in love with dancing. Henry knew she'd obviously retained a body memory of the dance steps, but also that it wouldn't have lasted forever.

It was an aggressive disease. Gorging on her memories. The most recent ones first, those from adulthood next, followed by her teenage years and finally those from childhood. And it wasn't just memories. Motor skills were included in the deal. She'd have lost control of her muscles. She'd have become bedridden. At some point her brain would've forgotten how to swallow. Like all of us, the first thing she learnt would've been the last to go. The doctor would've fed her on a drip, until finally, she suffocated, having forgotten how to breathe.

Henry tried to focus on the fact that she was spared such an end. Her identity stripped in this inverted order. It offered him little solace. And with all his recent worries he couldn't help but think this was the kind of journey he now faced.

The door was ajar but Sean still knocked. There was no response and he eased his way in.

'Not hungry Henry?' Sean went to take the untouched sandwiches.

Henry didn't reply.

'I tell you Henry,' Sean continued. 'You're all right. Some people in this place seem to think we're servants, that we're at their beck and call, 'Why isn't my dinner ready now?' I want, I want. Like babes throwing tantrums to get their own way. But not you Henry, no, you've always been decent.'

Henry remained silent.

'Shall we have a look at the news? You haven't watched it all day.' Sean switched on Henry's television.

The reporter spoke over what was now generic footage of the tsunami.

'Anthropologists fear that indigenous tribes may have been wiped out by the tsunami. The remote chain of islands, known as the Andamans and Nicobars, was one of the areas hit hardest. The hunter-gatherer societies that live there have had little contact with the outside world.'

The camera cut to a talking head, a small wizened Indian gentleman, in a battered tweed jacket. Introduced as Dr Manish Chandi, an anthropologist from Delhi University, he gave his expert opinion. 'Due to the remote nature of these islands it is hard for us to know how badly these tribes have been affected.'

The screen cut back to the anchor in the studio, 'In other news, the death toll across the whole of the Pacific rim currently stands at an estimated one hundred and sixteen thousand people.'

'Wow, that's pretty grim isn't it?' Sean said.

Still Henry didn't respond.

*

In all his years of people watching, there'd been several occasions where someone did an about face and looked right back at Henry, as if they knew. He was sitting in the lounge, reading the paper, facing away from the door, when he felt a boring sensation at the base of his skull. It made him want to turn around. However, as it hurt to look over his shoulder, he had to stand and shuffle.

When he saw Sean standing in the middle of the doorway, staring directly at him, Henry felt annoyed. He hadn't been able to create the same element of surprise. Sean walked across the room, slapping a piece of paper against his thigh, which he then presented to Henry.

It was a leaflet, with a loud red typeface that said, 'Seize the Day.' There was a picture of a young man, and in front of him an older man. It looked as if they were strapped together. The young man held his arms outstretched and the old man had his thumb aloft. They were skydiving.

On the inside page it showed a series of photos, a granny riding pillion on a burly biker's Harley, an old gent standing next to a vintage car, two silver haired women in an embrace. The leaflet posed the question. 'Is there something you've always wanted to do? Do you have an unfulfilled ambition?'

It was two weeks since Henry had chanced upon the photo of him and Maud dancing. He still didn't feel himself.

'What's that to do with me?' He held out the leaflet and snorted.

'Well, you remember Bletchley Park, the centre of code breaking, from the war, where they cracked all the German communications?'

'Of course I remember. You think I'm losing my marbles?'

'You know these days it's a museum – I thought you might fancy a day trip?'

Sean pulled out a second leaflet. 'Look, there's the Colossus Rebuild and the Enigma Collection. The dawn of computing, think how much you'd love it?'

Henry looked at this leaflet, at the tiny pictures of the first, room-sized, computers. They were feats of genius, truly amazing. A tingle ran the length and breadth of his scalp and continued down his spine. His heart kicked against his ribcage and he suddenly felt light headed. He thought he might need a sit down.

Sean helped him back into his chair, removed his glasses and knelt beside him. Henry caught his breath.

'No need to decide now,' Sean said. 'I'll just put them in your room. You can look later.'

'Don't bother,' Henry wheezed. 'I'm too old to be running around on wild goose chases.'

'Henry–'

'You never listen to me. I'm not going and you can't make me.'

The real reason was the war. One particular instance came back to him. One among many. He'd left his two mates and walked up the hill to his lodgings. Behind him he heard the footsteps. Stiff and brisk. His ears attuned but he didn't look round. Neither did he alter his pace.

He strained to hear any clues, any quickening of the feet following him. But the footfall had synched with his own. Firm and heavy, definitely male. And as he neared the brow of the hill the man called out, his voice coarse.

'Oi laddie, you just wait there, I want a word with you.'

Henry froze. He recognised the tone of authority. Just what he didn't need. Definitely a copper.

He strode up to Henry in his uniform, his buttons polished, his helmet and chin strap firmly in place. This wouldn't even be happening, Henry thought, if they'd given us uniforms.

'So tell me, if you don't mind, what's a young lad like you, able bodied, still got his arms and legs, some might say, in his prime, what's a lad like you doing here, in Stafford?'

Henry said. 'Sir–'

The policeman rested his truncheon on Henry's solar plexus.

'Now, when I see a lad like you, it gets me thinking, and I have to ask myself, how come he's not out there, doing his bit for King and Country? Eh? You one of them objectors, boy? You think you're too good for the war?'

'No Sir, I'm down the mine. We need coal to fight the war, all our battleships and the trains that keep our boys in munitions.'

'Work down the pit. Rather than fight Gerry. This better not be some fairytale.' The truncheon dropped to his side.

'No word of a lie Sir, I took the draft, I was ready to fight, but they needed men to work the mines, and my number was drawn.'

The next afternoon Henry booted up the computer in the lounge and searched for tsunami developments. The National Geographic website had a new article, entitled 'Did Island Tribes Use Ancient Lore to Evade Tsunami?'

The indigenous tribes, who still lived a hunter-gatherer life, and were threatened by Western encroachment and disease, had survived relatively unscathed. However, those who led more assimilated lives, having converted to Christianity and become horticulturists and pig herders, they were badly hit, with over ten thousand people missing and feared dead. The overall death toll currently stood at one hundred and eighty thousand, much higher than originally reported.

Henry wondered how the hunter-gatherer tribes had survived. Was there a link between this story and the one a few days after the tsunami, which reported how hardly any animals had died? There must be some rational explanation.

The article made reference to ancient folklore, and an acute awareness of the ocean, the earth and animal movements. There was also an aside made about one of their gods, Pulga, who, in their mythology, was responsible for previous cataclysmic floods.

National Geographic obviously couldn't find a convincing explanation. Henry decided it must've been luck; for once the tribes' superstitions had been fortuitous. He shut down the computer and told himself that this was a satisfactory answer.

It was a couple of hours before teatime, and as there was so little to do these days, no chess, no dancing, he thought he might as well head back to his room. As he stood he could feel aches and pains all over. In his right knee, in both of his hips, and all of his fingers. His whole body seemed to be in uproar.

Sean had left the leaflets on Henry's wheeled table. Henry let himself plop into his comfy chair and began to assemble his thoughts, while browsing the Bletchley museum's offering. It was romanticism. To suppose a connection between the majority of animals and a few indigenous tribes having survived the tsunami.

Similar to the coincidence of him dreaming about Maud's death on the same night she happened to die. These things didn't mean anything. They were just random occurrences.

All the same, there was a stark contrast with the German tourist video. Blithely standing on the beach, commenting on the craziness of a ten-foot wave as it rushed towards them. Such disconnection seemed to be a particularly Western problem. With all of the West's technological gains had people also lost touch with some intrinsic part of themselves?

The more he turned it over, the more he came to the conclusion that maybe his thought process did need the re-injection of some intellectual resolve. A trip to the birthplace of the computer revolution could be just the trick.

Henry spent the journey in the passenger seat of Sean's Fiat, a wheelchair jammed into the boot. He'd been persuaded it would be a good idea, just in case he got tired. Not that it bothered him in the least. To be going to Bletchley Park, to see the enormous, valve-driven, code breaking, Colossus computer. Part of the gargantuan effort involved in cracking Tunny, the cipher used by the Nazi high command. Henry couldn't remember ever being so excited.

That wasn't true. When he was five years old his father had cut down their oak tree. He said it was too close to the house. Henry cried at the sight of the stump and the sap. Several months later he noticed the new shoots, pushing up from the severed trunk. The tree that towered above their house, cut down to the height of his belly button, killed, he thought, by his father. And yet, there it was, still alive. He was fascinated. How could it be? By what magic?

Henry was equally amazed by his recall of the event. The image stood stark in his memory, even though he hadn't thought about it in years and years. The leaves, sprouting this way and that, deep purple and half unfurled. In his mind's eye he revisited their dark, almost malevolent, colour. An abrupt contrast to their tender, intricate veins. They were reaching out into the world, and now he couldn't help but think of them as being filled with hope and trust.

Sean gave the handbrake a hard yank. He muttered to himself, opened his map and traced the shape of a 'T' back and forth.

Henry was aware of a brief pause. Two options stood before him. The first was his predictable irritation when interrupted. The second was to stay with his excitement. He waited, didn't feel particularly perturbed, and so amused himself with their surroundings.

The main street was deserted of people. A couple of pigeons pecked around the varnished wood of an ornately carved 'Chawston' sign. At the other end of the village, outside the flint church, a big ginger tom paraded down the middle of the road, confident in the midst of his territory.

Sean looked up. 'It's no good Henry, for the life of me I can't see where we are. I knew I should have brought a better map.' Henry decided that was okay. He had no doubts. No underlying fear that he'd miss out.

'Sorry,' Sean said. 'I'm a bit distracted. Had to take my cat to the vet yesterday. She's been going a bit loopy of late. Fishing tea-bags out of the compost and eating them.'

Again, rather than be annoyed, Henry found himself turning to Sean as he continued.

'The vet said the tannin in tea bags is poisonous for cats. He said, sometimes, when they're as old as she is, they'll decide they've had enough.'

'Do you mind, can I ask if you're religious?'

Sean laughed. 'Good Roman Catholic boy, me.'

'And do you really believe?'

Sean looked at Henry and winked.

'I know you scientific types say there's nothing but this world, materialism and what have you, but to me, I don't know, it just seems that there is more.'

'What do you mean?'

'Okay, so fair enough I'm not the most charitable person in

the world, I've had my share of troubles, but I do try to be a better person. I know when I do wrong and I try not to.'

'How?'

'I can't really say, I suppose I just feel smaller.'

Henry put his hand to his mouth and cleared his throat. That pause again. A part of him felt like scoffing. Another part didn't.

'I'm sorry to hear about your cat.'

'I'm sorry about Eddie. And Maud. God, you've had a rough old time so far this year.'

Henry wanted to open up. To tell Sean about his dream on the night of Maud's death. But he couldn't. A wall stood in the way. Just the thought of talking about it and his mind spiralled into a panic. He quietly edged back.

To the left of the pigeons and the village sign stood the Church hall, a modern, orange brick construction. Two ladies with sensible hats and three-quarter-length coats walked out of the building and down its path. As they approached the main street Henry realised this was an opportunity. They might know the way to Bletchley.

He willed them to turn towards Sean and himself. And when they did just that he worried the handle of his window. It was tight and, in his bulbous hand, it jerked. As the women passed Henry had the window halfway down.

'Good morning ladies,' he said. 'You wouldn't happen to know which way we need to take for Bletchley Park?'

They did, and as Sean pulled away, Henry repeated the directions to himself.

'You old rogue,' Sean said at the edge of the village.

For a second Henry's annoyance reared up, but Sean was grinning and Henry allowed himself a smile. They were back en route, only twenty minutes to go, and he was still rather excited.

They turned into the Bletchley Park driveway and Henry's euphoria was overtaken by a ballooning exhaustion. He hadn't made such a long journey in the eight years since he moved into the home. Sean swung passed Bletchley Hall, with its amalgam of architectural styles, and into the car park next door. Henry looked over at the mansion's Anglican green dome. It was a long walk and he decided it might be a good idea to use the wheelchair.

Their guide was waiting for them in front of the mansion. She was a matronly ex-Wren in a sky blue twin set. Her handshake was firm and she introduced herself as Joan and said. 'There should be another group joining us, so we'll just hang on to see if they turn up.'

As three women walked over from the direction of the car park Joan looked at her watch and tutted. One of the women was tall with short spiky hair, which was dyed burgundy red. Alongside her was a petite Asian woman. Her hair was also cropped, and both of them were wearing trouser suits. Henry found the little and large effect off putting.

The third member of their group was a pale-skinned, fair-haired woman. She was younger, wore a flowing dress, and walked a step behind her two friends.

All three were chatting loudly.

The tall woman said. 'No, it's got to be in Hut 8.'

The other two burst out laughing and the Asian woman said. 'Yeah, he's such a geek-throb.'

Some things in the modern world Henry just didn't understand. He got the heartthrob reference, and of course, he knew who'd worked in Hut 8. They must've been fans of Alan Turing, the mathematician. But that made no sense. Why would they hold a flame for Turing, when he was both dead and homosexual?

The women nodded to Joan, Sean and Henry.

'Hello there.' Sean said, singling out the fair-haired woman with his smile.

The tour began with Joan telling them how she'd served at Bletchley during the war. She operated one of the Bombes. These were the electro-mechanical constructions designed by Turing.

Joan continued by giving a quick introduction to the history of Bletchley Park, with which Henry was familiar, having read all the books. How Admiral Hugh Sinclair foresaw the coming war and the wisdom of a location away from London, and purchased the house and grounds for the Government Code and Cipher School.

The linguists and mathematicians from the 'school' relocated in 1939. They initially worked from the mansion's main hall until the wooden huts were shipped in and erected. The continuation of the war and the expansion of Bletchley Park's activities meant that by 1941 construction had started on the larger brick blocks.

Then the Americans joined the war and at Bletchley, from 1943 onwards, there was very close cooperation between the American and British code breakers. So, Henry thought, if you wanted to find the heart of the 'special relationship' look no further than the vast amounts of intelligence the two countries exchanged. The surveillance of both the NSA and GCHQ had its roots in the secrets shared at Bletchley.

Joan beckoned them to follow her, pointing out Hut 4. It had housed Naval Intelligence, but was now commandeered by the café. Sean introduced himself and Henry to the fair-haired woman. Henry forgot her name instantly, as he was silently cursing Sean for not keeping up with Joan.

They stopped at the dispatch riders entrance, which consisted of a walled drive and two inbuilt sentry points. Joan described how enciphered messages were picked up by listening posts along the coast, transcribed and rushed to Bletchley Park. Again Henry knew this, but still, to be in the drive itself.

They went round the various outbuildings and semi-derelict huts, ending up at Hut 8, home to the cryptographers who worked on the German Enigma code. Due to the Museum's lack of funding, this was the only fully renovated hut. They went inside to see the mock up of Alan Turing's office, with his mug chained to the radiator.

Joan spoke about this and Turing's other eccentricities,

but ended with. 'Anyhow, to me he was always very polite.'

She went on to describe how Turing worked in reverse to crack Enigma. The principle being that out of one hundred and fifty eight million, million, million possibilities, it was easier to discount those that wouldn't work, leaving the few hundred that could be right.

Next they went to see the Bombes. The machines designed to carry out these calculations. According to Joan, there were three problems with being a Bombe operator. The noise, the heat and the smell.

At the end of an eight hour shift her ears rang, she was desperate to get out of her uniform and no matter how long she spent in the bath, she still stank of oil.

Henry was enjoying himself. He felt an affinity with Joan. She was a no-nonsense woman, brisk and to the point. There were things she knew that you'd never find in any book.

The replica Bombe was as large as the sidewall in Henry's room. It consisted of three rows of cylinders, each of which was three deep and twelve wide. They were basically large electro-mechanical calculators. Each cylinder mimicked one of the Enigma machine's three rotors, which had encrypted the original German message.

Henry knew the Bombes had driven Bletchley's assembly line approach to cracking Enigma and so he raised his hand. 'How many Bombes were in use at Bletchley?'

'By the end of the war, some two hundred.' Joan said.

'And did they improve Turing's original design?'

'Now that's a good question. Yes, they did add extra cylinders, so each Bombe could simulate twelve Enigma machines.'

Henry felt a flush of pride.

'But in truth, that was the main failing of the Germans,' Joan said. 'They had great faith in their technology. It was state of the art and they didn't believe it could be cracked.'

'Could you tell us,' the tall woman said. 'How many women worked at Bletchley, and what their roles were?'

'There were at least eight thousand of us, compared with

about two thousand men. And yes, they did give us all the menial jobs, but that's the way things were in those days.'

The woman laughed. 'At the cutting edge in so many respects, and yet…'

Joan continued. 'But we had our fun as well. There were dances and clubs. London was an hour away on the train. We were young and had no idea what the future held. There were lots of romances. Some friends of mine met here and after the war they got married. It was strange though, because the whole culture was don't tell, don't ask, they spent fifty years as husband and wife, but not once did they speak about what their jobs had been.'

The tall woman spoke again, much to Henry's irritation. 'There was a lot of that wasn't there? People whose parents died thinking they'd done nothing useful during the war.'

Henry's annoyance melted instantly. It was a situation he found all too familiar. His father had always lampooned him for a war spent down the pit. Not that he, or any of the other Bevin Boys, were given a choice. Something his father never took on board, that it was a lottery dictated by their National Service number.

The Museum of Computing was next. Joan strode on ahead, not turning to see if the group were keeping up. Henry told Sean to hurry. He didn't want to miss a word of how these huge electro-mechanical calculators became digital computers.

At the entrance Joan explained how a young mathematician, Bill Tutte, had devised a method for cracking the cipher used by the Nazi commanders. At Bletchley this code was known as Tunny. Henry had read about Tutte, and he was impressed by Joan's knowledge of the subject.

It wouldn't be long before they got onto Tommy Flowers, the Post Office engineer who designed and built Colossus, the world's first semi-programmable computer, which had made the cracking of Tunny workable. It was reputed to have shortened the war by two years, saving millions of lives.

After the war, Churchill's insistence upon secrecy meant that

Flowers' achievements went largely unrecognised. But as far as Henry was concerned, Tommy Flowers would always be the real hero.

Joan led them through. Sean bumped the wheelchair over a door ledge. Henry cursed and shifted uncomfortably. The Colossus Rebuild resembled several large aluminium shelving-units. Stacks of panels were filled with knobs and switches. Banks of cables connected these to the rows of flashing lights.

Joan pointed out that it was a fully functioning machine. A rebuild of the first computer. Henry thought it looked like a Boy's Own Adventure for boffins.

And they were in luck, that afternoon it was up and running. The room was warm and stuffy. A ticker tape whirred. It ran on pulleys, within a cast iron frame, nicknamed the Bedstead. Henry looked for Colossus' optical reader, knowing that the tape passed through this at thirty miles an hour. It was where Colossus read the coded messages.

In contrast to the whirring, Colossus also emitted a monotonous beat. It reminded Henry of the machine stamps when he'd been an engineering apprentice. His gaze flicked around the room. The rhythm corresponded to the blink of the output lights.

Tutte devised the method. His section head, Max Newman saw how it could be mechanised. But still, it was Flowers, the engineer, who built the world's first computer.

A scholarship boy from the East End. A post office engineer from the days when the postal service ran the telephone exchanges. Unacknowledged during his lifetime, unable to talk about or build upon his creation.

Henry had always been interested in facts and dates. The mechanics of parts and pieces. But to be sitting in front of the working rebuild, he felt a strange reverence. If he'd been a church going man, he wondered whether it would count as a religious experience.

The physical impression of the whole machine. Its obvious

weight, Joan said over a ton. The noise and heat it generated, the intricacies of its working processes. From the ticker tape input, to the final decoded message.

Henry could easily see how Turing had gone on to found the science of artificial life. It must've been somehow akin to witnessing the birth of a new species.

Joan explained the finer details of how Colossus was operated. Henry was all ears. Until the tall woman spoke again. 'I'm writing a paper on the role of intuition at Bletchley Park.'

Henry wondered if that was what people on Internet forums meant, when they said someone was completely random.

'But that's just stupid,' he couldn't help himself. 'They were mathematicians.'

'Henry.' Sean said from the corner of the room, where he'd been whispering with the fair-haired woman.

'The thing is,' the tall woman continued. 'From what I've read, the development of Colossus involved several intuitive leaps. I was just wondering if the people here at Bletchley have looked into that at all?'

'Not that I'm aware of, dear.' Joan said.

The tour ended with Colossus and so for the rest of their time Henry asked much more practical questions.

As Joan wrapped things up Henry was surprised to see the tall woman approach him. Sean was still flirting with the fair-haired woman, which Henry once again found very frustrating. His means of escape denied.

'Hi, my name's Toni,' the tall woman said.. 'Could I possibly buy you a cup of coffee? I'd like to ask you some questions.'

'About?'

'You know so much about the place, I thought it'd be interesting to have a chat.'

Sean must've overheard Toni.

'Of course, we'd love to join you for a coffee.' Henry felt Sean's hand on his shoulder.

'That'd be nice,' the fair-haired woman added.

Ten minutes later, Henry sat at a table in Hut 4, the café.

Toni came over with a tray of drinks and sat opposite. It was only as she began to talk about her paper that Henry realised Sean and the other two women had walked passed their table and taken one in the far corner. He felt a sense of dread and hoped she wouldn't go on and on about this intuition thing.

Toni didn't waste any time. 'Were you here during the war?'

'No.'

'Oh, I just thought, maybe…'

Henry suspected she was humouring him.

'You don't mind if I ask what you did do during the war?'

She held his gaze and reached out. Her fingertip fleetingly stroked the back of his hand. It was a very feminine gesture. The kind of thing he remembered Maud doing.

But still, he wasn't telling her about his war as a Bevin Boy. The way it'd shaped his life, limited its scope. The fact that afterwards he hadn't been allowed to enrol in college, or go back to his apprenticeship.

'Nothing that exciting. You wanted to talk about intuition.'

Henry wondered which was worse, to have achieved something monumental, but be unable to build upon it, or to have the potential to achieve ripped from you by an unlucky draw.

'I was wondering, maybe you could help me with my paper? You know I said before, about the role of intuition in Bletchley Park's code breaking.'

'How do you mean?' Henry said.

'Well, how about Jack Good?'

'What about him? Another brilliant mathematician.'

'And the Offizier message that was doubly enciphered?'

'I haven't heard of that.'

'Good was baffled by his failure to break a double cipher, but then in a dream he saw the settings inverted and when he tried it the next day it worked. He literally broke it in his sleep.'

'Well, these days don't they make a lot of noise about the subconscious?'

'And what about Bill Tutte?'

'Yes? He was handed the Tunny key and the associated documents, all the failed attempts to crack the cipher, and told to see what he could do with it.'

Toni continued the story. 'Its stream of characters seemed entirely random. But Tutte found a chink. The frequency of zeros and ones in a message could be turned into a percentage. This statistical average demonstrated that the randomness was a mirage. From there he reverse engineered the entire structure of the machine. The question I'm interested in is how exactly did he do that?'

'Isn't it obvious?' Henry said. 'He was well trained, not to mention extremely gifted. It was a great intellectual feat, yes he had some luck with where he began his search, but there was nothing mystical about it.'

'But why him? What about the others, who spent three months trying to crack it. They were no slouches. Why didn't they see what he did?'

'Who knows, his experiences? His care and dedication? A natural aptitude?'

'And Max Newman?' Toni continued. 'A theoretical, pencil and paper, mathematician. Why would he instantly see that they needed a digital counting machine?'

'The whole thrust of the age. Of the war. Turing had already broken Enigma with a mechanised approach. Sorry, but in that there's no surprise.'

'Okay, so how about Flowers?' Toni said. 'He saw the first attempt to build such a machine and knew he could do better. His intuition told him that the electronic valves would be reliable. Bletchley Park didn't believe him, but even so he persevered with his convictions and built Colossus.'

Here Henry knew he was on home ground. 'Without doubt, that was his experience. He used valves on the telephone exchanges and knew they were dependable.'

'Okay, but wasn't he summoned to Bletchley because he was also an expert on the old technology, relays? It's like it was meant to be. No one else in Britain could've done that.

Without him the war could well have been lost. Even you must admit it was fortuitous, the right man, in the right place, at the right time?'

Henry smiled. Their conversation was more enjoyable than he'd expected.

On the return journey Henry was lost to his thoughts. Did a connection exist between his dream and the so-called intuition displayed at Bletchley? Had his experience somehow allowed him to have that dream?

Surely, knowing a friend had died, sensing the moment they passed, when you weren't there and hadn't been told, that had to be different. If he hadn't experienced it himself, he would never have believed it. Even now the whole thing seemed made up. In what kind of world did such things happen?

Sean had walked into his room to break the news. Henry already knew. He didn't want to believe it, and yet he had no doubt. She was gone. How could he know that from a dream?

These were the questions he'd done his best to avoid. Now, finally, he was face to face with them.

Sean slowed as they approached a crossroads. 'You've got that million miles away look. You thinking about the museum?'

'No.'

'Oh. Right.'

In the background a song played softly on the radio. Sean hummed a phrase from its melody. He leant on the steering wheel, checked left and right at the junction. He squinted and scratched the bridge of his nose. As he pulled out a four-by-four cut them up. He swore, apologised, and continued humming.

To Henry he seemed completely oblivious to himself. And yet he was a decent bloke. His intentions were good. He was a young man. His earlier flirtations no longer felt so important.

Henry wanted to talk. He had a sense of being overwhelmed. He needed to get these thoughts out in the open.

He made his decision. He'd tell Sean everything.

Only the prospect made him apprehensive.

'Actually…' Henry's mouth dried up; his saliva felt more like an adhesive.

Sean offered him a bottle of water.

Henry drank and tried again.

His mind froze. What could he use as an opening gambit?

Then, an idea broke the surface. Completely against the current of his worldview. Maybe the genius of Tutte and Flowers didn't correspond to his dream. If so, had he been looking in the wrong place? Wasn't there a more likely candidate?

The answer gushed from Henry. 'Those animals and indigenous people who survived the tsunami. The media spoke about the animals having a sixth sense. They referred to long-standing beliefs. They wheeled out animal experts.'

Sean frowned.

Henry continued. 'But when it came to the indigenous tribes, the idea of a sixth sense was forgotten. They survived because of other factors. They were attuned to the movements of the animals. Or their myths told them to move to the mountains when the ground shook.'

Sean pursed his lips before speaking. 'But what's that to do with Bletchley?'

'No, listen, what if the tribes also had a sixth sense? What if that's something that animals and humans share? After all, we are mammals. Wouldn't such a sense be more accessible to indigenous people? While here in the West, with all our hi-tech distractions, should we be surprised if it gets drowned out?'

'I don't understand.' Sean grimaced.

'Well, those German tourists, standing and watching the oncoming tsunami, let's be honest, they didn't show too much insight.'

'I get all that. Foresight, clairvoyance and the like. Of course, some of us are more sensitive. I just thought you'd be excited about Bletchley.'

'But it's all connected.'

'Sure.' Sean changed gear with a crunch.

Henry winced at the grind of metal on metal. 'Yes really, in the café, me and Toni were talking about Tutte and Flowers.'

'Who?'

'The mathematician and the engineer who built Colossus. You must remember the big computer?'

'Okay, be sarcastic.'

'We were discussing the extent to which their work was guided by intuition.'

Sean snorted. Up ahead there was a lay-by. He snatched at the indicator, lurched the car to a halt and turned the engine off.

For a minute they sat in silence as the passing lorries made the car vibrate. Next to them was a bin overflowing with empty Styrofoam cups and discarded crisp packets.

Sean exhaled long and hard. Henry was confused. Had he said something wrong?

'Look Henry, I'm not smart like you. All I want to know is did you enjoy yourself? This is my day off. Was it worth the effort?'

Henry's stomach twisted in on itself. He looked away from Sean. He stared at the swollen bin and wondered why he never learnt. He thought about how best to broach an apology.

Sean touched his arm. 'Why don't you tell me Henry? What's been going on? You've not been yourself since Maud passed.'

Henry's chest trembled.

'I had a dream, the night she died,' he said. 'I woke up knowing she'd gone.'

'No surprise there. You should have seen you two dance.'

'But I thought I was going senile. How can you be so matter of fact?'

Sean gave a short laugh. 'Years of practice, mate.'

Henry looked at him and frowned.

'Like I said before, all this,' Sean swept his arm in a gesture that included the car, the lay-by, the bin and the trees beyond. 'For me there's more to the universe. Things happen and we can't explain them rationally. We don't see all the connections. It's a living, breathing world. And like it or not, we're part of it. That's the hardest step, my old Grandpa used to say, learning to accept ourselves.'

'But…' Henry didn't finish.

Sean turned to him. 'I get what you're saying, about the tsunami. You're asking if there's a similarity between their escape and your premonition?'

'I suppose I am.'

'Henry, I can't say for sure, there could be. One thing I know. In all my years at care homes, all the residents I've worked with, you may have your moments, but you're definitely not going senile.'

Sean put his hand on Henry's and smiled.

Henry sat there and stared out of the window. He felt giddy. Like when they were winched up from the pit, and the chain slipped. That moment of weightlessness. Followed by a jaw-crunching jolt. And then a flood of relief. The chain had held.

It was breakfast time and Henry was on his way to the dining room. At the end of the corridor, by the top of the stairs, he could hear a couple of the care staff cooing and aahing.

Suddenly Mandy, one of the carers, came racing down the corridor.

'Quick, Henry, go and see.' She rushed passed him.

As he continued along the corridor he heard Mandy calling to other residents and members of the care team.

'Come and look.'

Henry rounded the corner and there at the top of the stairs, staring out through the huge plate glass window were Sean and Karen, the home manager.

'Look, Henry.' Sean pointed.

Perched on the roof opposite them was a Heron. She stood on the apex of the roof, resting on one leg. Absolutely motionless. Streamlined. The height of elegance.

Along from her a territorial crow flapped its wings and

hopped closer. Sean said he heard it squawk. The heron seemed oblivious.

'What's he doing, I've never seen one out this way?' Sean turned to Henry.

'Not he, she. Her lower mandible's longer than her top one. That means she's female.' He could just make out the familiar tapered shape.

'What's a mandible?'

'Her beak,' Henry smiled. 'She's looking for water. Because its winter, the fish go deeper, they're harder to find, and she has to travel further afield.'

While correct, Henry felt this explanation was lacking. Something about the heron's presence was eerie. Everyone's reaction made that clear. But what was it?

He recalled the awe he'd felt sitting in front of Colossus. There was a similar sense of bearing witness. At least seven or eight of them stood watching the heron. Both residents and staff. The home's routine had been brought to a halt, ruptured by this incursion from the wild.

Karen walked in the direction of her office. She got to the door, but came back to continue watching.

'I don't know why I'm so fascinated.' She said.

Henry's reply was immediate. 'Because she's beautiful.'

'That she is.' Sean gently cupped Henry's elbow.

The heron spread her wings. They were surprisingly wide. One beat and she glided into the air. A second beat and she cleared their side of the building. Henry's last glimpse was of an outstretched wing and two trailing legs.

Slowly the other residents continued on into the dining room. Karen went back to her office. Mandy headed off down the corridor. Sean offered Henry his arm, and for once Henry accepted.

NIAGARA FALLS

James Wall

It's not yet dawn and I'm on the M62 heading for the airport. I've not been here since Ali. My eyes feel heavy but I'm not tired. There's been nothing on the road for some time so I welcome the yellow streetlights when they come, wishing they could be here all the time. They bring a warm glow against the harsh September night. When they're gone and I see a car's lights in the distance, I smile, glad of some company, and feel empty when I can no longer see them in the rear view mirror. I can still sense her beside me, the shape of her at the edge of my vision. She's the one who's supposed to keep me awake on long journeys but, now, she's the one who is sleeping.

It was a year ago that I 'found' her on Facebook, and twenty years since I'd last seen her. She must have only recently signed up; I had been looking for a long time. In her profile picture, her hair was longer than I remembered, and she was smiling at the camera. She still had that slight nervousness in her expression that I had always loved. I searched for her status but there was nothing completed. It doesn't mean anything, I told myself.

I hesitated before adding her as a friend. What if she rejected my request, or just ignored it? I couldn't settle while I waited for her reply. Stupid after all this time I know.

My post to her was short and casual, but it took me half an hour to get the words right, going back over what I'd written, changing it repeatedly: 'Hi! Great to see you on here! What have you been up to over the last twenty years?'

I remembered her as slim with short brown hair. She often wore a red and white baseball jacket around uni. That makes her sound boyish but she was anything but. She had expressive eyes, accentuated by her long eyelashes. Her skin was smooth and clear. She caught me looking at her once in a lecture on the poetry of Wordsworth. She smiled and then turned back to the lecturer at the front. I learnt to become more adept at observing her after that and would quickly look down at my notes when I detected a slight move of her head in my direction. I did have girlfriends during that time, none of whom I remember that clearly. One was semi-serious – but I could never lose the 'semi' part. Not with Ali around. And she was seldom without a boyfriend. None of our 'in-between' partner periods coincided, although I often wondered whether I should ask her out anyway. But something always intruded when I had built up the courage to do so.

We had the same friends, went to the Union bar, same pubs, same cafés. For years afterwards I remembered the night we all went out to celebrate our finals. I was the only one sober. I wanted to remember this time, to keep it in my mind, and replay it whenever I liked. Was I the only one who realised what that night meant, that I wouldn't see her again? I had thought so at the time. Ali wore jeans and a checked blouse. Her top button had come undone during the evening and exposed the top of her bra, the soft dip of her cleavage. I liked to think she'd done this for me. She was still seeing Sean then (they finished a few months later I subsequently discovered). A few went out for curry and chips after closing, but Ali and Sean said they were heading off. There were about ten of us, and I waited in line for a farewell hug from her. She felt so warm, her body slight and delicate against mine as we held each other. It crossed my mind to say how I felt, to tell her to forget about Sean and be with me. She whispered something just as the others were laughing loudly at a joke, but I couldn't make out what she said.

'Come on,' called Sean, and I felt her pull away.

'What did you say?' I asked.

I don't think she heard me. She just looked to the ground, her hands in front of her, and Sean put his arm around her waist and they left. He must have known how I felt. It must have been obvious to everyone.

Like a scattering of birds after gunshot, we all separated after uni. I kept in touch with Pete but only for about six months. Not deliberately; other things just got in the way. The last time we met up, he told me that Ali had broken up with Sean.

'Why don't you go after her?' he said.

I shook my head. I wasn't going to make more of a fool of myself than I already had. She could tell how I felt and hadn't responded. But by then, I'd started at Harrison's and had just met Freya.

Even after she and I were married, I often had a few minutes alone with Ali in my mind. I would close my eyes, think of our hug and breathe in the smell of her skin – the scent of soap and lemons. With time it became harder to remember, the memory fading like an old photograph left out in the sun. I wondered what she was doing now, whether she was married, or had any children. Freya and I had two boys, Adam and George, eighteen months apart. Beautiful, lively boys. I see them most weekends now, and for longer during the school holidays. It was difficult for a time, but now I think they have forgiven me for leaving.

I could have married again. I met Katherine at work soon before I left there to try teaching, and we lived together for five years. She wanted to, but I said I wasn't sure. After Freya.

A convenient excuse.

She held me in her arms as she said, 'Don't let one bad experience put you off. I'm not Freya.'

I smiled but was silent. You're not Ali, I thought without wanting to.

She supported me while I trained, and again when I realised I hated teaching and left the school. She was lovely when she said that I would find something else, something I loved. But she couldn't quite stop letting me know that she was not my ex-wife, a flush of red appearing on her chest whenever she did, a faint tremble in her hands. Even at the doorway, her belongings already moved into her new home, she said so again before slowly placing her door key in my palm.

In my small flat, I refreshed the page every few minutes after sending my message to Ali. Maybe she was just being polite in accepting my request. Never had any intention of actually communicating with me. But then, after a few days, she replied, saying she'd been away with work. She said it was great to hear from me. I read over the words again and again, looking for a latent message in them but finding nothing.

She'd moved to York a few years ago, she said. I sat back. She'd been so near for all this time and I didn't know? Didn't she remember I was from around here and said I would be coming back? I felt my shoulders sink. I told myself that it was a long time ago and not to overreact.

I responded quickly, suggesting that we meet up as I lived so near.

I didn't hear anything back for days, and chastised myself for being so hasty. Did I appear too keen? Finally she replied and we arranged to meet at a café in York, near the Minster.

It was early autumn, and the remnants of summer lingered in the air. After tentative kisses in greeting, we sat outside with our coffees and cakes, although I felt too nervous to eat. She wore a blue dress and burgundy flat shoes. Her bare legs had a hint of colour but it didn't look as if she'd been in the sun for long. No summer holiday then, I surmised. No boyfriend to go with? I surreptitiously checked her left hand and saw no wedding ring.

A toddler from the next table escaped from his mother as she was putting her coat on and ran over to us, giggling.

'Hello,' said Ali, bending down to him, his big eyes staring back at her as he grabbed onto the edge of the table to steady himself. 'What's your name?'

'Come on, Isaac,' his mother said, walking over and feeding the child's arm into his coat sleeve. She lifted her head towards us. 'Sorry about that.'

Ali and I caught each other waving away her concerns simultaneously, as a couple may do, as if we'd been together for years.

We reminisced because that is what we had. At first. She'd forgotten about Sean, when I reminded her of him. She laughed and shook her head. A mistake, she said.

She told me about her marriage to Philip, and how it had ended a few years ago. She worked for a while teaching English as a foreign language in Eastern Europe, primarily Lodz in Poland and Bruno in Czechoslovakia. She missed it or rather missed the idea of being there. There was a large department at York University and she was tasked with developing the foreign student intake, many from Japan, so she had visited there a few times.

The Minster clock struck one and she apologised, gathered her bag and stood up. It felt as if I'd only just sat down. In a way I had.

'I have to get back to work. Didn't realise what time it was.' There was a flatness to her voice.

Her cheek felt warm as I kissed her goodbye. I watched her climb onto her bicycle and ride back towards the university, her long dress flapping in the wind behind her as if waving goodbye.

Later that afternoon, I nervously suggested dinner.

She accepted in the evening, and I couldn't settle in the days leading up to it – our first meal together. I found myself pacing around my flat, or staring out of the window and reliving our brief meeting. I was unable to think of anything else. We met at a Japanese restaurant I'd never been to before. As the waiter showed us to our seat, I was sure Ali left behind a trail of turned heads marking our route.

The wine came; we clinked our glasses together and caught ourselves smiling foolishly.

'Feel like a teenager,' she said, her eyes filled with light.

'I know,' I said. 'We were only just out of our teens the last time we saw each other.'

She shook her head. 'Frightening.'

As I asked if she had any children, an image of Adam and George smiling at me entered my mind.

'No,' she said, dipping her head, and dabbing her mouth with her napkin. She quickly asked about me, and what I'd been doing.

I hesitated for a second, caught a little by surprise at her reticence but didn't pursue it, hoping there'd be other times to talk, before I told her about my jobs, the aborted careers. She said I was very brave not settling for just anything.

'Or stupid,' I said. 'There's not settling for just anything or just not settling.'

She laid her hand on mine. So light and soft, I could feel the grubby, tired layers rising from me.

At the end of the evening, over coffee, after two bottles of wine, she said she wished I'd asked her out at uni, and that she'd whispered to me during that last night out about keeping in touch. She thought I hadn't reacted, so had assumed I wasn't interested.

My chest tightened into a fist, her hand in mine. 'No, no, not at all.'

Please don't say that, I thought to myself. If I'd known what she'd said that night, things would have been so different.

Afterwards, we saw each other several times a week,

sometimes more; we spoke daily on the phone, and often texted. We even sent each other letters, which felt old fashioned among the millions of emails I could sense around me constantly. It was as if we were becoming fixed in our own, separate time where nobody else existed. I listened out for the post each day, and on hearing it flop onto the mat, raced to tear her letter open, reciting out loud from my favourite Wordsworth poem, 'My heart leaps up when I behold' as I did so.

It was a couple of months later that I mentioned a holiday. She didn't answer at first, and I was worried that I'd been too rash.

'Where?' she said at last. 'I'm not keen on beach holidays.'

I smiled. 'Nor me. How about Canada?' She started laughing. 'What? Why is Canada funny?'

'I've always wanted to go there,' she said, and cupped my cheeks in her warm hands before kissing me softly on my lips.

The high wall is on my left. It always marks the approach to the airport for me, and I know there's not long to go now. I open the window and welcome the cool air in, feeling it over my forehead and against my hot cheeks. A trickle of sweat runs down by my ear and drips from the side of my jaw.

We stayed at the Sheraton in Toronto and visited the usual tourist attractions: the CN Tower (she grabbed on to me when we gingerly stepped onto the glass floor in the observation platform and looked down), the harbour front where we sat out as the sun slowly started to descend, and took a ferry out to the islands.

It sounds silly now but I wasn't that keen on seeing Niagara Falls.

'It's just a big waterfall isn't it?' I said.

'We can't come all this way and not go to Niagara Falls.'

She clung on to my arm and I turned and kissed the top of her head. I can still smell the tang of her shampoo in my nostrils now. Orange blossom and lemon balm.

The sun was shining the day we went to see the Falls,

and as we looked down over them we saw the white spray rise up and create an ephemeral rainbow in the air. We bought tickets and both wore the blue plastic, semi-transparent ponchos we were given. We boarded the Maid of the Mist and held onto each other as the boat slowly approached from the side and moved along the length of the horseshoe. There was a constant roar from the millions of litres of water crashing down – the spray rising up before us, continually replenishing itself, over and over.

The guide said that some people had thrown themselves off in the past, and a few had even survived. One went down in a wooden barrel. I looked up to the top, watching the water tipping over and falling, imagining the barrel plunging down to the wash below, breaking apart as it hit. She followed my gaze and held me tighter. We were so close then that it was as if our edges had become blurred, as if our bodies were no longer separate. I blinked and eventually had to close my eyes, the sun was so brightly reflected from the Falls. It felt as if the water in the air was enveloping us then, not like rain but a constant presence, a natural state of being, like a baptism. We kissed, her lips soft and damp with spray, and I listened to the constant rush around us, how it blocked everything and everyone else out.

It was a night flight back home. I thought we would find it easier to sleep. The only lights that were on were small and dim. The hum of the plane's engines surrounded us, interrupted only by occasional hushed voices. There was a free seat on our row on which we put our bags, and we sat under the blue airline blankets as we watched a film.

I must have dozed off as I woke with a start. I looked over to Ali; she was still sleeping beside me. Her hand was on my forearm, and tensed just as the plane shuddered from turbulence. I rested my hand on hers. She'd said she hated flying and I wasn't sure whether she'd remembered to take the pills to calm her. The turbulence continued and I sensed her body stiffening. An uneasy murmur passed through the plane like a strong breeze, and I thought of Niagara Falls, the spray rising up, its watery fingers reaching out. Ali jerked in her seat and I turned to see her body tense as she clutched at her arm. I thought at first that she was having a bad dream, brought on by the plane shuddering, and that she'd settle back to sleep in a minute. But she didn't. She was awake; she couldn't catch her breath. She grappled at her arm and her face lost its colour. Her eyes grew larger; there was fear magnified in them, as if they contained something both bright and terrible. I jumped up and cried out for a doctor. A stewardess ran over and put out a call on the intercom.

'Ali! Ali!' I kept standing up and sitting down in quick succession, desperate for what I could do to stop this and make everything right again.

I was ushered out of the way by a slight, thin man who pushed in next to her. My view was partly obstructed by stewardesses but I could make out his movements becoming more and more frantic.

He was over her now, pumping at her chest. He stopped to give her mouth-to-mouth, and pumped again. Soon, his face was red and his brow was glistening. After a time he sat back and all was still. All I remember hearing was the sound of the engines, how the cold air outside battled to push through them.

I press lightly on the brakes, but there's no hard shoulder for me to stop so that I can think about turning around. I've tried so many times to reverse our time together in my mind, to put it back to how it was before I sent her that message, but I can only get as far as my coffee cup filling up from my mouth with each backward sip at our first meeting near the Minster. Or making the little boy stagger away from us instead of towards.

Back in my flat, after all the questions, the forms signed, I kept the curtains closed, unplugged the phone, and left only for the funeral. I just wanted to sleep, but could only catch an odd hour, if that. Whenever I did, I woke with a start, and pushed my hand out in search of Ali next to me, all of it starting again as soon as I realised she wasn't there, as soon as I realised I was alone.

A few weeks later, I went out to the local shop for some bread and milk, a vague inkling of hunger in my stomach for the first time I could remember in a long while. My heart sank when I bumped into Katherine. She said I looked awful.

'Thanks,' I said.

I told her briefly what had happened. A weak heart, they'd said. Could have happened at any time. That must have been why she had no children. Would have been too much for her. Katherine placed her hand on my arm.

Afterwards, she kept coming round, bringing me food. It was her idea to go for walks now and again.

'I wish I'd left her alone,' I told her. 'She'd still be here if I had.'

'Don't think like that.'

I tried, but it didn't make much difference. The same thoughts kept revolving around my head. Oddly, it was Katherine who persuaded me to get away. I could think of nothing more I'd like to do than be away from home. She said it would do me good to be somewhere different. In the end I said I would and I told her I'd booked to go on a short break somewhere; she didn't ask where and I didn't tell her. She offered to drive me to the airport but I told her no.

I pause at the car park barrier. Last chance to turn back. My hands fall from the steering wheel onto my lap. In my mind's eye, I see Ali laughing. We were in a café on Queen Street a few days before we left. I can't remember what she said now, but the laughter grew inside us and we couldn't stop. For that short period of time, when it had all clicked into place and I'd found her again, I'd never been so happy.

I find a space at the far end of the car park, amongst the rows and rows of other cars and sit remembering Ali next to me the last time we were here. I can see her teasing me about being so organised as to make a note of the row we were parked in. We kissed softly, slowly, before getting out and walking to the bus that would take us to the terminal for our flight, my fingers reaching for hers in the gap between us.

I'm startled by a knock on my window. A man is asking me if I'm alright.

'Couldn't help noticing,' he is saying. 'We saw you as we were coming back to our car with our luggage.' He gestures behind him but then stands upright.

'Thought you were staying in the car,' he calls to someone I can't see.

'I'm OK,' a woman says.

She comes into view. She is wearing a dark blue smock dress. There's a bump, not big, but noticeable.

'Janice took a turn just before,' he says. 'We was sitting and doing the breathing the doctor had told her to do and then she said you hadn't moved.'

They both bend down to my eye level, and she strokes her stomach.

'You alright?' she asks.

'Yes, thank you,' I say. 'Very kind of you to ask. Both of you.'

I watch them through the window and imagine this must be how a child perceives adults. It makes me feel small and alone.

She cocks her head. There's a redness that rises briefly about her throat and then dissipates.

She turns to leave but then stops and asks, 'Where are you going?'

I glance to the passenger seat, at my messenger bag slumped there containing a book of Wordsworth poems and the plane tickets. 'Canada,' I say. 'Niagara Falls.'

She looks at her husband. 'We've always wanted to go there.'

I smile, and they return to their car.

I don't remember much of the flight or the transfer to the hotel in Toronto. I don't remember the row where I parked the car, and haven't written it down.

I'm up early the next day for the trip, sleep having visited me only intermittently during the night. It's not long before I'm wearing the blue poncho again and I'm standing alone at the back of the Maid of the Mist boat as everyone else gathers at the front. There's the roar of the water, but it doesn't seem as loud this time. As we reach the bottom of the Falls, I retrieve the letter I'd written to Ali from my bag and run my fingers over her name on the envelope. I hold it between my fingers for what seems an age, my hands over the railings, before I finally let go and watch it flutter in the breeze, and drop silently into the bright and churning water.

HAY. PEE. AH. WRIST

Jonathan Pinnock

A. P. R. Ist. Ist: doesn't make sense. Ist isn't a word, stupid. Try again. Ape. E. Artist. No, no, no. Wrong, wrong, wrong. Hay. Pee. Ah. Wrist. Hay. Pee. Ah. Wrist.

Hold on to that.

Hold on tight.

Six hives. Six colonies. Sixty thousand bees in each colony. So that's three hundred and sixty thousand bees. One thousand lots of three hundred and sixty. One thousand times round the circle.

And of those, how many men, eh?

Maybe a thousand drones in each colony, tops. The rest, all women.

Must be a drone then. Just a boring drone. I AM MAN HEAR ME DRONE. Drone, drone, drone. Bzzzzzzzzzzzzzzzzzzzzzz.

Hay. Pee. Ah. Wrist.

Six hives. Six colonies. Three hundred and sixty thousand bees.

Things to remember, number one: check the colony every week for new queen cells. New queen comes along, and half the colony pisses off with her. That's the trouble with queens.

You can only have one at a time.

And I'm just a drone, drone, drone. Bzzzzzzzzzzzzzzzzzzzzzz. What was that song? 'Wish I was a buzzy buzzy bee'? I ask you I askyew askew askew Arthur Askew NO NO NO Arthur Askey, Arthur Askey as in Askey's wafers. Wafer thin. Wafer thin mints. Wafer thin mince. Mince pies spies I-Spy I spy with my little eye –

I don't want to open my eye.

Hay. Pee. Ah. Wrist.

They're National hives. Not Commercial hives, National. Hold on to that. Ten fourteen inch by twelve-inch frames plus a dummy board, Hoffman frames, Hoffman Hoffman Philip Seymour Hoffman Samuel Hoffman thereminist wheeeooowheeeooo Beach Boys Good Vibrations good vibes vibes vibraphone who was that fat bloke who played the vibraphone? Patrick Moore! Sky at Night, knights in armour amour propre French letters condoms condominium dominion Dominion Theatre, London STILL SHOWING THAT FUCKING QUEEN MUSICAL –

Hold on tight.

Is he OK? Dad? What's wrong with him?

Hay. Pee. Ah. Wrist.

I can wait all day if you like. There may be three hundred and sixty thousand of you, but I can wait all day.

She kept on at me, you know. Why don't you ever take me somewhere nice? Like that thing in the West End. Mamma Mia? No, not that, silly. That thing with Freddie Mercury. We Will Rock You. Rock you, rock you, rock-a-bye-baby in the tree top, tree top, tip top, tip top condition, conditioner, hair conditioning, air conditioning, Curved Air, remember that multi-coloured vinyl that used to fall apart?

Curved Air. Now there was a band.

Not Queen.

Don't even talk to me about Queen.

Cos I'm just a drone, remember? Drone, drone, drone. Bzzzzzzzzzzzzzzzzzzzzzzz.

Hey! Mate! You all right over there?

Hay. Pee. Ah. Wrist.
  Hang on to that.
  Hang on tight.
  Should have used the smoker. Calms them down, see? Should have used the smoker. The smoker smoker all night toker, I'm a joker I'm a joker I'm the joker I'm Heath Ledger I'm a legend I'm a hero BECAUSE I'M THE FUCKING KING OF BEES.
  There is no King of bees.
  Only a Queen.
  We will we will we will rockyourockyourockyou.

Mate! Do you need some kind of help?

Hay. Pee. Ah.
  Hold on tight. Hold on tight to your love. Who was that? ELO ELO ELO 'ello 'ello 'ello what's all this ear then? Ear wax, Mo' Wax, wax on wax off, fighting without fighting DO NOT DESPISE THE SNAKE BECAUSE HE HAS NO HORNS.
  He may become…
  What the fuck was he going to become? I should know this. No, it's gone.
  Was I really more interested in my bees than her? Was I really? She didn't like the honey. Said it tasted of sick. Why bother spending all the time arsing about with my hives when you can buy a jar at Sainsburys for two pound fifty? You just do it so you can dress up in your stupid fencing suit. OK, have it your own way, I'm not going to wear the suit today, right?

Dad, he's moving. Dad, d'you think we should get someone? He's covered in them!

Hay. Pee.

Keep breathing, whatever you do. Keep breathing. Breathe in breathe out. Every breath you take. Every move. Ha. Hahahahaha. Oh, that's too funny. Too funny. If only I could laugh. Of all the bands to think of now. The one with that tosser on bass.

Sting.

Fucking Sting.

Hay.

Hay.

Ay.

EVERYTHING CHANGES, NOTHING PERISHES

Tim Sykes

I shudder to contemplate what would have come to pass were Malcolm not an entomologist – and a brilliant one at that – though of course we'd not have known.

Angus had phoned on the Tuesday evening to inform me of Father's passing. I drove down from Edinburgh the next day. The monotony of motorway travel was a welcome analgesic to the rawness of memory. Landscapes merged into landscapes, hills into fields, woods into suburban jungles. I passed twenty or thirty identical service stops. In time I was murmuring their mantra, 'Petrol 102 / Diesel 108', and when an aberrant '111' flashed into view it startled me like a Zen paradox.

I noticed that the young lady driving the car in my mirror was singing along to her radio. Her wholehearted mime captivated me and I contrived to stay just in front of her for miles. There came a moment when I was compelled to overtake a caravan. I waited for her Fiesta to follow but never saw her again. Gone too was Father, the celebrated 'poet in stone'. Yet he had never been quite with us, but instead hovered over us, casting quite a shadow.

It was late afternoon when I came into Oxford. I'd not been back for years. The streets were familiar but I didn't recognise the turn-offs until they were upon me. As I scanned the road ahead the great shoulders and spidery gait of Angus came into focus. He had evidently taken the train up from Paddington.

I pulled over.

'Stephen.' He gave my hand a short, tight clasp. 'We can go straight to the undertakers. Malcolm is already there… What the bloody hell is that car doing? If you're going to turn, woman, take the turn!'

I believe she may not have seen Angus shaking his fist.

We found Malcolm downstairs in the Visitation Room, gazing into the box. He nodded to us then went on looking. I stepped forward. Father's face used to remind me of a temple on a hill. In death its facades had been marble clad, and in a manner thus perfected.

'Father's estate won't be particularly complicated,' said Angus. 'As you know, he bequeathed his collection to the University. They've agreed to manage the house.'

He went upstairs to speak with the undertaker. Malcolm remained still. Eventually he too left. Oh Father, face on a hill, turned to white stone like one of your busts…

Angus had started shouting at someone. He was almost screaming. I went upstairs.

'You have bugs in your brain, Malcolm! They'll run you out of the college! I'm minded to assist them. Have you totally lost touch with reality in that ivory tower?'

Angus took a heavy breath. He had spent his anger. There was silence.

Malcolm turned to me. He was as phlegmatic as Father had been.

'Father isn't dead,' he said. 'He's pupating.'

He glanced at Angus and added, 'I appreciate this is rather a lot to take in.'

The three of us returned to the Visitation Room. The thing was, our Malcolm was indisputably one of the finest entomologists of his generation. And not given to clowning. With his usual verbal economy he showed us the clear indications of an exoskeleton forming beneath Father's skin. There were many organisms, he reminded us, which, as it were, 'shut down' in the midst of their life cycles (for instance, the heart of the larval form of some Arctiidae species actually stops in freezing weather). And there was no evidence of the preliminary stages of decomposition, which ought to have set in hours ago.

It *was* rather a lot to take in.

'We must get him home,' Angus said at last. Indeed, it wouldn't do for the old man to be entombed when he was done metamorphosing.

Angus straightened out the undertakers with an ease that suggested the inconvenience would not harm their ledgers. Within half an hour a hearse was following us back to Father's.

I stayed on at the house. Angus had business to attend to back in London. Father's mahogany cocoon lay in the conservatory. Malcolm dropped in from time to time to inspect his specimen, which was indeed exhibiting no signs of putrification, and had encased itself in a crystalline film. Father's giant cat – more an elderly, ginger sheep – would occasionally collapse on me, refusing to budge until my legs went numb. But most of the time I was alone with the house, the reflections and the sculptures.

So my childhood home was to become a museum. High-minded visitors would glide from room to room. They would courteously sidestep one another and thoughtfully gaze at Father's furious, craggy visages. They would picture the Great Man at work in this very house, and tingle at his proximity. They would not see Father's sons keeping out of his way. They would not see the three of us rioting quietly in the living room while he worked in the attic. They would not see us, home for school holidays forty years ago, lying on our beds, plotting dreams onto our ceilings. I had wanted to read philosophy but turned into a lawyer. Angus was mad about astronomy but went into money. Malcolm was dreaming of stag beetles even then. Malcolm was always the same.

All of Father's busts and reliefs depicted either antique Greeks or the Common Man in a bus queue. Each class looked equally disenchanted with his lot. In later life I came to understand the austere beauty others saw in them. And it can't have been easy to 'live in the grip of a compelling vision of existence in absurd flux', as one catalogue put it. I tend to doubt that Father's insight encompassed an awareness that his own life would follow quite so absurd a sequence of mutations as larva-pupa-imago. He may have enjoyed the irony.

It was in the process of boxing up his library that I came upon Father's sketchbooks. Wedged between Jung and, yes, Kafka, were fifteen inches of numbered brown spines smelling of old leather. I realised immediately they would be of immense value to scholars. They contained page after page of meticulous studies for his sculptures, including the three pieces that now belong to the Tate. Sometimes he would add a terse caption, such as 'Apollo & Daphne, Hampstead Heath' or 'superego in vortex'.

I turned one page and gasped out loud. Before me was a sketch of the three of us as boys. Angus must have been around seven and Malcolm ten. We were lolling over each other on the old sofa. Father had captured us in our joyful brotherly mischief. I couldn't recall Father ever stepping foot in the living room. I couldn't imagine having been so nakedly happy in Father's presence. Yet he must have been there.

The following page made me weep. There we were again, now sleeping, pristine in our beds. It is the tenderest image I have ever seen. Father was faithful to each interlocking eyelash, the warmth of our cheeks, the vulnerable sweetness of our unconscious selves. But on the very next page that pupating bastard petrified us. There we lay in precisely the same positions, now rendered in his characteristic, angular style. Our skin was textured like granite and into our sleeping features he had cut disappointment, pain and experience.

On the morning of the third day Malcolm observed that Father appeared ready. Angus rushed back to Oxford. We sat expectant in the conservatory. Hours passed. Angus grew agitated and started checking his watch. Finally he shouted at Malcolm for sitting too still and went into the living room.

At dusk it began to rustle.

'Angus, he's coming out!' I called.

'I can't move. The cat's sitting on me.'

There was a moment long enough for Angus to wrestle the beast, then hurried footsteps into the conservatory. We were bathed in purple evening light.

A crack had appeared in the chrysalis. We bore the coffin into the garden, in case Father on freeing himself flew or scuttled into the conservatory window. By now there were glimpses of something downy and hurried. It chipped at its redundant shell, gradually forming a circular hole where Father's crown had been. Pale hairs pushed at the aperture. Father's new form emerged.

Its wings were astounding. Twelve feet in span, a pale green that seemed to catch more light than the other colours in the garden. Its face was recognisably Father's, though softened, almost angelic in transformation.

'Father,' I said. 'Do you know me? I'm Stephen.'

It looked into my eyes. I could not discern whether he recognised me. He emitted a rapid series of clicks, a language that none of us could comprehend. He rotated his antennae, which were the size of ferns. Perhaps he wished to perceive us better or to feel out his changed world. Then our transfigured father opened his wings, rose into the sky and flew off in the direction of the moon.

We stood in the garden, breathing in the honeysuckle and jasmine. Angus was the first to speak.

'Let's go for a walk.'

We followed him inside.

The three of us had been lying on the grass for hours, taking careless swigs of Angus's scotch. We'd not done this since we were students. The midsummer air over Christ Church Meadow was full of insects and stars. Between them, Malcolm and Angus could have named them all. I think none of us wanted it to end, though the blackbirds were already singing. We knew we'd not be together again. Not like this anyway. Indeed, Malcolm died suddenly just two years later. Angus, in the middle, drained the whisky, tossed the bottle and pulled us into an embrace.

'Father…' he said, 'Wasn't Father a splendid imago?'

UNTHOLOGISTS

Gordon Collins has been a market risk analyst in London, a maths lecturer, an English teacher in Japan and a computer graphics researcher specialising in virtual humans. He has three different degrees in mathematics as well as an MA in Creative Writing from the University of East Anglia. He has been published in *Riptide Vol 3*, *Danse Macabre*, *Infinity's Kitchen*, *Liar's League* and the *UEA Creative Writing Anthology 2010*. His story *Even Meat Fill* appeared in *Unthology 3*.

Alexandros Plasatis is an exophonic writer undertaking a Creative Writing Ph.D in the UK. He has a short story published in *Overheard: Stories to Read Aloud* anthology (Salt, 2012). He is currently working on his first novel.

Daisy Lafarge (b. 1992) studies in Edinburgh where she writes and attempts to resist acquiring more houseplants. Her writing has appeared or is forthcoming in The *Scrambler*, *HOAX* and *Berfrois*.

Chrissie Gittins was born in Lancashire and lives in Forest Hill. Her first poetry collection is *Armature* (Arc) and her second is *I'll Dress One Night As You* (Salt). In 2013 Paekakariki Press published her third pamphlet collection *Professor Heger's Daughter* in traditional letterpress with 7 original wood engravings. Chrissie's short story collection is *Family Connections* (Salt). Her radio plays include *Poles Apart, Starved for Love, Life Assurance* and *Dinner in the Iguanodon*. Her three children's poetry collections are all Choices for the Poetry Book Society's Children's Poetry Bookshelf and two were shortlisted for the CLPE Poetry Award; she has made an hour's recording of her children's poems for the Poetry Archive. Bloomsbury published her new and collected children's poems *Stars in Jars* in 2014. Chrissie has received two Arts Council Writers' Awards, a Hawthornden Fellowship, and awards from the Author's Foundation and the Oppenheim-John Downes Memorial Trust; she is included in the British Council directory of UK and Commonwealth writers. www.chrissiegittins.co.uk.

Neil Campbell is from Manchester. He has two collections of short stories, *Broken Doll*, and *Pictures from Hopper*, published by Salt, and two poetry chapbooks, *Birds*, and *Bugsworth Diary*, published by Knives, Forks and Spoons. His first novella, *Sky Hooks* is now available as an e-book from Salt. A new chapbook of short fiction, *Ekphrasis,* is also available from Knives, Forks and Spoons. @neilcambers

Matthew Temple is currently looking for new ways (and new people) to turn his words into moving image, performance and visual art. He lives in London. *Kiss On A Thread* was shortlisted in a contest run by theNewerYork Press in the USA.

Roelof Bakker was born in the Netherlands and lives in London. He is the founder of Negative Press London and editor of *Still* (Negative Press London, 2012), which was runner-up for Best Mixed Anthology at the Saboteur Awards 2013. *Strong Room*, a collaboration with artist Jane Wildgoose, was published in 2014. His story *Red* appeared in *Unthology 5*.

Ailsa Cox's collection, *The Real Louise and Other Stories*, is published by Headland Press. She has also published stories in many other magazines and anthologies, including the *Warwick Review, Katherine Mansfield Studies, Overheard: Stories for Reading Aloud* (Salt) and *Best British Short Stories 2014* (Salt). She lives in Liverpool and teaches at Edge Hill University.

Georgina Parfitt is from Norfolk, England. She recently graduated from Harvard University and now works as a freelance writer all over the place, writing journalism, blogs and fiction. She has been published in *The Atlantic online, Plain China Anthology of US College Fiction*, and *Atticus Review*.

Robert Anthony is a writer, a musician and artist who lives in Brooklyn, New York. He's published in a variety of journals, most notably experimental fiction in *Tight,* poetry in the latest issue of *Kaffeeklatsch* (UK), and has poetry coming up in *Edge* (US). He's also released several albums of electronic and experimental music in the US and the EU as *Sleep Museum*. He lives halfway between a green park and a green cemetery, mid-way between the laughter of children and peaceful graves.

Luke Melia works in London, and writes fiction in his spare time. In 2011, *The Temp* was shortlisted for the Crime Writer's Association's Debut Dagger Award. In July 2012, *The Skedaddler*, a piece of US Civil war fiction, was most highly commended in the Tom Howard/John H. Reid Short Story Contest and is published on the Winning Writers website. In October 2013, his short story *The Application* was highly commended in the Highland and Island Short Story Association (HISSAC) annual competition and is published on the HISSAC website. He is currently drafting several new stories for a debut collection.

Victoria Hattersley lives in Norwich and works in publishing. She started writing properly in 2013 after years of prevaricating in various ways. She is now writing short stories in-between working on her first novel.

Graeme Finnie is a writer who lives in Glasgow. He is a graduate of the University of Glasgow's MLitt in Creative Writing programme. His work has appeared in *From Glasgow to Saturn*. He was long-listed for the Fish short story competition and short-listed for the Bridport Prize in 2014.

Simon Griffiths is from Walsall and has lived in Birmingham and Norfolk. *Stalemate* is his first published story and like many aspiring writers he has found semi-gainful employment in a variety of professions, from juggler to chef and from Amazon associate to new media artist. He is currently working on a novel.

James Wall is a novelist and short story writer. His work has previously been published in the *Best British Short Stories 2013* anthology, *Tears in the Fence, The View from Here, Prole* and in *Matter Magazine*. He was shortlisted for the Bridport Prize in 2010, and has an MA in Creative Writing from Sheffield Hallam University.

Jonathan Pinnock is the author of the novel *Mrs Darcy versus the Aliens* (Proxima, 2011), the Scott Prize-winning short story collection *Dot Dash* (Salt, 2012) and the bio-historico-musicological-memoir thing *Take It Cool* (Two Ravens Press, 2014).

Tim Sykes thought about writing for nearly 20 years. In 2013 he finally started. His first story is published here. Tim studied Russian and lived in St Petersburg in the 1990s. He is currently writing a cycle of stories that draw on his wanderings in Russia and Russian literature.